FOR HER HONOR

The Gentrys of Paradise

HOLLY BUSH

A heartfelt and deserved thank you to Jenny Quinlan at Historical Editorial for the gorgeous covers she creates for my books, making the visions of my characters a reality.

CHAPTER 1

Winchester, Virginia
April 1873

HE MISSED THE TASTE OF FOOD. HE MISSED THE TEXTURE OF rare roast beef, and the tang of a béarnaise sauce smothering it. He missed the smoothness of mashed turnips and the snap of a fresh bean from the garden. He missed the anticipation of a meal and a wine to complement it. Adam Gentry cut a bite of the pheasant breast on his plate, put it in his mouth, and looked up at the cook eagerly awaiting his approval.

"It's delicious and prepared perfectly," he said and forced a smile. "Thank you."

"I'm so glad you like it, Mr. Adam," Mabel, the Gentry cook for the last twenty years, said and hurried to the door that led to the kitchens.

He ignored the silence in the formal dining room of his family home at Paradise Stables, as there was nothing to say, was there? He sliced small pieces of meat and the candied beets on his plate and chewed until he could swallow. He didn't believe he would know if Mabel had changed out the pheasant for a book binding or a piece of pine bark. But it had been months, over six now, since his life had changed, and he was certain it would not suddenly or magically change back to happier days.

"Adam?" his mother, Eleanor Gentry, said, drawing his attention from his plate.

"Yes?" he replied, looking up at her, the matriarch of the Gentry family with his father gone now more than four years.

"Olivia has been asking you some questions," she said and smiled warmly at him. "You were concentrating on this delicious meal and didn't hear her, no doubt."

Adam turned his eyes to his sister sitting on his right beside her husband. Even though their one-year wedding anniversary had just passed, Olivia and Jim Somerset still gazed at each other as if it were the very first time they'd ever seen each other and recognized their love. Especially his brother-in-law. He'd known him since Jim's father, the local farrier, had begun servicing the Paradise horses when they were young boys. Jim had taken over those duties years ago when his father passed. Adam glanced at him now and he was staring at Olivia with a look that was nearly worshipful. Perhaps it was.

"When will we have the first foals?" Olivia asked.

Adam thought about last year's foaling and what a happy time it had been. Josephine had come from Washington and stayed for nearly ten days. He could look back and identify those days as the ones when he realized he'd fallen in love with her. "George thinks the first will drop in two weeks."

"How many, Adam?" his younger brother, Matt, asked from where he sat beside his wife, Annie.

"Eleven."

"York has done his duty and more it seems!" his mother said with a laugh. Everyone at the table chuckled except Matt, who shouted, "Yee haw!"

It was all he could do to keep himself in his chair as he had a nearly overwhelming desire to punch his brother in the face until all of his teeth were gone. He filled his crystal tumbler from the whiskey decanter in front of him, drank it down in one swift swallow, and smacked his glass on the gleaming walnut table forcefully enough to shake the pewter candlesticks on either side of the flower centerpiece. Olivia reached out and steadied them. When he looked up, everyone was busy cutting their food and generally looking elsewhere, other than Matt.

"Leave a little of that for Jim and me." He nodded at the decanter.

Adam continued to pick at his food and refilled his tumbler again. When dessert was served, he stood abruptly and picked up his glass with one hand and the decanter with the other. "I'll be in the office, Mother."

He pulled a random book from the shelves that lined two sides, floor to ceiling, of the large room he used to do the Paradise Stables business. It was originally designed to be a library, but his father had loved the room and put a large cherrywood desk between the two tall windows to keep track of the accounting and correspondence, although his mother participated in that as well when his father was alive. Now, it was his desk.

He put his glass down on the felt pad and rifled through the mail stacked on one corner. The bills he handled efficiently still, but he'd put off reading the letters about the family's investments and offers for other business opportunities. He knew he needed to open them and determine what was to be done, whether to increase or begin an investment, or withdraw funds, or even to research a new prospect, often with Matt's, Livie's, or his mother's help. But he hadn't even opened many of the letters, and the ones he had lay in another stack as they had been for several months.

Adam seated himself in an overstuffed chair in front of the fire and looked at the title of the book he'd pulled. *Agriculture Practices for Growing Rice*. He opened to the first page and thought this book might be just the thing to bore him to death, so much easier than a bullet to the brain. He'd contemplated that scene in his head for a brief but vivid minute after it had finally become real to him that Josephine Wright would never talk to him again or make love to him another time.

The days after receiving her brother's telegram of her illness and traveling anxiously to her bedside he'd been in a stunned shock. It couldn't be happening. She'd had some stomach discomfort over the weeks before but nothing serious, at least that's what she'd told him. When the pain had become so severe that she'd fainted in the foyer of her Washington townhouse, her brother Darien, Adam's friend from Franklin College, had taken her directly to Columbia Hospital for Women.

Josephine had been quickly diagnosed with appendicitis. A surgeon with experience in the procedure had been scheduled to arrive the following day as he was out of town visiting relatives. His hurry to his hometown had been for naught. Josephine's temperature had spiked, and the doctors believed her appendix had ruptured. She'd died three hours later with Adam and her brother each holding one of her hands.

She'd told him, though, she'd told him before she drifted off to a fever-induced comatose state. She'd kissed his hand and told him she loved him. That he was the love of her life. He'd fought tears and smiled at her and told her, as he'd been saying for months, that he loved her. He couldn't believe at the time that she would actually die even as she weakened, visibly shrinking before his eyes. He was certain, absolutely sure, that some miracle would occur, that she would rally, that the doctor would arrive, that there was some other explanation for her pain. But at two in the morning her heart just stopped beating.

As had his.

It was unfortunate he didn't die.

Tears rolled down his cheeks as he filled his glass from the decanter again, his hands shaking, his lip trembling with the remembrance. He laid his head back against the chair and closed his eyes.

* * *

OLIVIA TOUCHED HER BROTHER ADAM'S SHOULDER AS SHE TOOK the empty crystal glass from where it was wedged between the side of the chair and his leg, but he didn't stir. She cupped his cheek in her hand, smelling the liquor odor from his clothes and breath.

"Can you get him upstairs, Jim?" she asked her husband.

"Go on up, Livie," he said.

"I can help you."

Jim shook his head. "Go to bed. I'll get him settled."

He waited until he heard his wife make her way up the steps. He pulled his brother-in-law to his feet and put Adam's arm around his neck. Jim slipped his arm around his waist hoping to propel him forward, but Adam's legs refused to cooperate. He began a slow slide down Jim's side. Jim pulled him up again, bent forward, and put him over his shoulder. Adam was a big man, but he was half a head shorter than Jim and fifty pounds lighter. It was no hardship to carry him.

Jim went up the steps and walked silently down the hallway toward Adam's suite of rooms. His mother-in-law's bedroom door opened.

"Do you need help?" Eleanor Gentry asked as she knotted the tie on her robe.

"No ma'am. I'll see to him."

* * *

ADAM WOKE THE NEXT MORNING, HIS MOUTH FEELING AS IF someone had stuffed it with straw, and his head pounding. It hurt to move even the slightest bit. He lay very still, waiting for his stomach to stop rolling, finally sitting up on the side of the bed, his elbows on his knees and his face in his hands. He didn't hear the door open, didn't even realize there was someone in his rooms with him until he looked through his fingers and saw a pair of boots. They were massive, heavy leather, and under a pair of dark thick work pants. They were attached to his brother-in-law, Jim Somerset.

"Morning," Jim said.

Adam smelled coffee. A rich aroma that would either cause his stomach to revolt or settle in short order. He opened his eyes and watched the steam rising from the cup. He sat up straight, took a deep breath, and reached for the coffee with a none-too-steady hand. He took a slow, tentative sip of the hot liquid and let it burn its way down his throat. His stomach seemed to be once again under his control. He looked up at his brother-in-law and burped.

"Must have been so engrossed in what I was doing last night, I didn't realize I'd had a bit too much to drink. Thanks for the coffee," he said and took another tentative sip.

Jim Somerset dropped down on his haunches, putting him at eye level with Adam. He shook his head.

"Most nights you manage to stumble up the steps, but last night I carried you up here over my shoulder as I have done four times over the last two weeks."

"Should have just let me sleep wherever I was."

Jim shook his head again. "Mrs. Gentry and my wife don't care for that much. They think you should be in your bed."

Adam looked at the clock on the table. Nearly noontime. "They should just let me alone," he said with a shrug.

"I do my best to keep them away from you. I chased Livie from the library last night before I hauled your ass up the steps. Unfortunately, your mother heard me coming down the hallway and opened her door. She offered to see to you. I told her I'd take care of things, thinking you'd not want your mother yanking off your pants at your age."

Jim didn't talk much. That trait had nearly kept him from marrying Livie, his being too hardheaded and taciturn for a decade to tell her that he was mad about her. When he did string together a sentence or three it was of some importance.

Adam looked up from his lap to Jim's face. There was no pity there, thank God above. He didn't think he could take pity. But there was some impatience, which was odd to see on Jim's face, especially as Jim was the same age as Matt, more than five years younger than Adam. And Adam was the head of the family now, had been since his father's death.

Adam went with bravado as it seemed he had no other recourse. "Don't put yourself out on my account, Somerset. You're not my keeper."

Jim stood, stretching out to his full six feet and four inches. "I don't do it for you, Adam, although I have a sincere sympathy for you. If anything happened to Livie, I'm not sure how I would live through it. I do it for your mother and your sister and your sister-in-law and your brother. I do it for Mabel, too. They love you. It's tearing them apart watching you drown yourself and all of your brilliance and potential in a whiskey bottle night after night. Livie is haunted by it."

Adam looked up and, to his mortification, felt tears in his eyes. "I don't know what to do, Jim. I just don't know what to do," he whispered. "The whiskey helps me forget and makes me remember, too. I'm caught tight in a trap of my own making."

"My mother grieved deeply when Father died. I asked her one day how she was doing. She told me she was putting one foot in front of the other with a conscious effort and that she hoped one day she would not have to be so deliberate about everyday living but that for now, it was the only thing keeping her sane. Just the everyday living."

"Deliberate," Adam said and looked up. "I must be deliberate in order to not put a gun in my mouth."

Jim nodded and turned to the door. "George has been talking to me and Matt a lot about the foaling. I think he's feeling as if he were on his own as stable master this season."

Adam watched his brother-in-law leave his rooms, pulling the door shut softly as he went. He licked his lips and felt the tears rolling down his face. He let himself have a good long cry, heaving and shaking and blubbering, calling out her name, Josephine, his love, struggling for an even breath, and finally pushing the panic down to a manageable level. He took three long, deep breaths and knew that he must continue on living, as he was alive, and find a way to do regular things, find routines without the help of a bottle of whiskey. He went to his bathing room, filled his tub with hot water, and peeled off his underclothes, smelling the liquor on his skin. It very nearly made him vomit.

THE SOMERSET HOME, WINCHESTER, VIRGINIA

"ARE YOU SICK AGAIN?"

Emmaline Somerset looked up at her sister Betsy, who was looking at her with sympathy and concern from the vanity in the large bedroom they shared on the second floor of the Somerset household. Emmaline was on her side in their bed, facing the wall and taking deep, slow breaths. She looked over her shoulder and forced a smile.

"I'm fine. Something just didn't agree with me at last night's dinner," she said. "Go on down. Tell mother I'll be there in a minute."

But the door to the bedroom opened a crack and her mother peeked in. "Emmaline? Are you ill?"

She shook her head and shrugged. "Those pickles just didn't agree with me last night and I ate so many of them."

"Are you sure, dear?"

"I'm fine," she said. "Don't fuss. I'll be down in a minute."

Her mother closed the door and Emmaline rolled over quickly to vomit in the thankfully empty chamber pot that was still in their bedroom, even though they'd had inside plumbing for as long as she could remember. She was taking slow breaths and shivering when Betsy handed her a wet rag to wipe her mouth.

"You didn't eat any pickles last night, Emmaline. I was seated beside you. You've been sick for nearly three weeks. I think you should tell mother and go to see Doctor Carter."

She looked up at her sister and shook her head. "No. I'm not going to the doctor's."

Betsy went to the door of their room and stopped. "I'm worried about you, Emmaline. Very worried."

Emmaline watched her sister leave and pull the door closed behind her. She sat up on her bed, her hand on her stomach. She'd never really had troubles before this. Oh, her mother nagged her because she was twenty-two and had no interest in marriage. Had never met a man she thought she could tolerate for more than a few hours at a time. And now that Betsy was stepping out with Edwin Crawper, Emmaline was officially left behind as a younger sister headed in the direction of the matrimonial altar. But those were small matters as long as she kept her sense of humor. *This* was not a small matter.

How did she get herself into this mess? But she knew how. She knew. And she knew that she was going to have to tell her mother very soon. As much as her mother could be silly sometimes and occasionally scatterbrained, Emmaline loved her dearly and knew she was loved in return. Imagining the disappointment on her mother's face when she told her was more than she could bear. She stood, swaying on her feet, holding onto the bedpost as she pulled on her petticoats, willing her mother's face from her mind's eye.

* * *

EMMALINE WAITED UNTIL EVERYONE HAD LEFT THE DINING room table after their luncheon had been served and cleared. She'd moved small amounts of food around on her plate making it appear as though she'd eaten. She had not. Her mother hadn't noticed as she was too interested in Edwin Crawper showing up at their door in his Sunday suit, twirling his hat, and asking if he could speak to Betsy alone. She couldn't ruin this day for her sister with an announcement that would cast a shadow on the whole family. It would be best if she waited until after Betsy was married. But that wasn't realistic. She was already four months along.

Emmaline was panicking as she sat and listened to her mother talk about dresses and dates and invitations. She was taking short breaths through her mouth and staring straight ahead.

"Emmaline! Are you listening to me?" her mother said, breaking her from her thoughts.

"What? Oh. Oh, yes."

"Emmaline, dear, you are white as a ghost! What is the matter? Are you still feeling sickly?"

She nodded.

"Why don't you lie down for a while. I'll tell Jane to help Helen in the kitchen."

Emmaline opened and closed her mouth. She wasn't sure she could form words even if she was certain she could speak. How would she tell her? How would she tell her sisters and brothers and sister-in-law and brother-in-law? She remembered when Marabelle Winston's cousin delivered a son six months after her wedding date. It was talked about for weeks at every sewing circle and church meeting as if she hadn't married a perfectly respectable man and delivered a child that looked so much like his father there could be no denial that even though she'd anticipated her vows, it had been with her future husband. Emmaline clearly remembered the lecture from her mother to her and Betsy and Jane.

"Do you girls understand what has happened?" Louise Somerset had asked them,

red-faced.

They'd all nodded, although looking back it was clear she hadn't quite understood.

"Marabelle's cousin Eliza had *relations* with a man before she was married. That is a sin before God most of all, but it is also a blight on that poor young lady's name that will never be removed."

"Why is Eliza only to blame? The man was there, or it wouldn't have happened," Emmaline had asked.

"Because it is a woman's duty to guard herself. Guard her . . . body and her chasteness. Women's innocence is expected."

"They are married now, though," Jane had said. "It all worked out for the best."

"But that is my point, girls," Louise had replied. "It does not always, or mostly, work out for the best for the woman involved."

"That's not fair," Emmaline had said.

Louise had turned to her and spoken sharply. "Of course, it isn't fair. Many things are not. But unmarried women who deliver a child are almost always looked at as less than respectable *and* unmarriageable. It is uncomfortable for the girl's family as well. Even Marabelle's mother, Eliza's aunt, was being asked questions at the Ladies Meeting last week."

"What could Mrs. Winston be guilty of?" Emmaline asked. "She is an aunt only, and Eliza's family lives in Middletown."

"Mother's point is that the actions of one family member can cast a shadow on other family members who are perfectly innocent, even obviously innocent, yet it is the way of things," Jane had said softly.

Emmaline looked up sharply from her memories as her mother shook her shoulder gently and leaned close to her face.

"Emmaline, darling. What is wrong? You are crying."

"Mother. I have to tell you something," Emmaline said and felt light-headed as she did. She clung to the edge of the table, twisting the lace cloth. "I . . . I'm . . ."

The door to the dining room flew open and Betsy came in, hand in hand with a blushing Edwin Crawper. "Mother! Edwin has asked me to marry him and I have agreed!" She began to cry as Louise gathered her in her arms.

"I am so happy for you!" Louise said and pulled Edwin close and kissed his cheek. "A new member of our family! How wonderful!"

Jane and their longtime cook, Helen, came from the kitchen and both hugged Betsy. The youngest Somerset, Phillip, wanted to know what all the commotion was and shook Edwin's hand. Louise dispatched Phillip to tell his sister Nettie to bring her husband, John, and the children on Saturday night for a celebration and told him to hurry back as he'd have to go to Paradise to invite his brother, Jim, and Olivia, as they lived with Olivia's family while their new home was being built.

Emmaline smiled, as she was really very happy for her sister and thought the tall, shy Edwin perfect for her. But she was dangerously close to bursting into tears, something that would alert her family that there was something wrong with her other than some bad pickles as Emmaline never, ever cried. She'd cried when her father died, though, as she'd sat alone in the woods behind the house, leaning against an oak tree. No one had seen her, and she'd wiped her face thoroughly before going back into the house.

CHAPTER 2

Emmaline woke with a start, her mother and Nettie leaning over her, Nettie fanning her with towels and her mother wiping her forehead with a cool rag. She was in her bedroom on the bed and beginning to piece together how she came to be lying there in her good dress. Betsy and Edwin's party to celebrate their engagement! Now she remembered. But why . . .

"You fainted, darling," her mother said softly, worry lining her face.

"Is something hurting you?" Nettie asked. "Your stomach? Your head?"

Emmaline looked at her eldest sister. There really was no turning back now. It had to be said. She was not well. "I need to speak to mother alone, Nettie."

Nettie's brow wrinkled, and she cocked her head to one side. "Yes. Yes, of course. Let me know if you need anything." She glanced to their mother.

"Most everyone will be leaving, Nettie. Please see the guests off for me," Louise Somerset said as she continued to stare at Emmaline. She swallowed visibly.

Emmaline heard the door close and sat up with her mother's help. "Please sit down beside me, Mother."

She sat down slowly and gathered Emmaline's hands into her lap. She was bracing herself for whatever came next, Emmaline imagined. But was it possible to brace yourself against this sort of thing? The humiliation? The worry? Some whisper of joy faintly heard and somehow adding to the weight of the guilt she carried? She looked up from her thoughts, realizing she'd been staring off, while her mother waited for some disastrous news. But it was surely better for her mother and for everyone before they knew her news, yet it could not wait a minute longer.

"I'm going to have a child."

Louise stared at her, smiled faintly, and shook her head. "Who is having a child?"

"I am. I am going to have a baby."

"How can that be?" Louise asked softly and touched her cheek. "You're not married."

Emmaline stared at her mother and licked her lips. "I'm not married but I am with child, Mother."

Louise shook her head but then her eyes widened and darted from side to side. Her mouth opened and closed. "Emmaline? That means you have had . . ."

But her mother couldn't complete the sentence. Emmaline took a deep breath and looked away. "I am with child."

"Who is the father? He must be made to marry you at once!" Louise whispered.

She shook her head. "No. There will be no marriage."

"But you must!"

"I will not. Don't ask me again."

"I will have Jim speak to the young man. Who is he?"

"No one will speak to him. I will not marry him. I won't compound one mistake with a second."

Her mother was red-faced and breathing quickly, wringing her hands in her lap. She was as angry as Emmaline had ever seen her.

. . .

"AND WHAT HAVE I LECTURED TO YOU GIRLS, TIME AND AGAIN? What were you thinking, Emmaline? What could you have possibly been thinking?" Louise stood then, paced the room, stopping to turn to the bed. "What will you do?"

Emmaline swallowed. "I am hoping you will continue to allow me to live here. At least until the child is born."

"Allow it? You are my daughter. You will stay right here," she said and then whispered. "But there will be difficulties."

"I know it will be hard for everyone, that's why I'm going to ask Aunt Madge if I can live with her after the child is born. At least I would be away from here and I could make up a story to tell Aunt. Something about a husband who has died or left me. There will be less talk if I'm not here to remind everyone of my . . . situation."

"We cannot think of those things now. How far along?"

"Nearly four months. I will keep to my room and the house and perhaps we can forestall the gossips, but we will have to tell the family." Emmaline looked up and hardened her chin, trying desperately to not think about the look on Jim's face, or the disappointment in Nettie's eyes or the embarrassment in Betsy's.

"Yes. We will, and we had best go do exactly that while everyone is still here. They are all worried about you, especially Betsy." Louise took a long breath, her shoulders slumping. "We will tell Nettie and Olivia and Betsy and Jane together. Nettie can tell John and I'll tell Phillip when it's absolutely necessary. Olivia can tell—"

"No. I will tell Jim myself."

Her mother nodded. "Come along then if you are feeling up to it."

Emmaline stood. "I just want the telling to be over. I've made myself ill with worry and am terrified I've hurt this child."

Louise walked to her and held her hands tight between them.

She looked away for a moment or two and finally turned to her. "I love you, dear. We will do the best we can."

* * *

EMMALINE WATCHED THE BLOOD DRAIN FROM NETTIE'S FACE and the confusion on Betsy, Olivia, and Jane's faces grow as she told them her news as they sat together in the chairs in front of the fire, Jane sitting on a cushion at her feet. Her mother sat on a chair near the window, staring out at the street.

"How far along are you, Emmaline?" Nettie asked.

"Nearly four months."

Nettie swallowed and stared back at her. "Brunsville," she whispered.

Emmaline shook her head, forestalling any more questions or comments. She looked at Olivia. "I would like to tell Jim myself."

"Of course. I'll say nothing until you've spoken to him."

She looked at Jane and Betsy. "I'm sorry to bring this down on all of my family but mostly I'm sorry to dampen the excitement over your engagement, Betsy, and you, Jane, may suffer consequences that are unstoppable."

Betsy shook her head but would not meet her eyes. "Edwin will not judge you. If he did, he would be the wrong husband for me, wouldn't he?"

Emmaline smiled as much as she was able, but she could see the worry, and maybe anger, in Betsy's face even as she spoke those foolish words. What *would* Edwin think?

"It will turn out for the best," Jane said and stood on her knees in front of Emmaline, reaching for her hands. "It will all work out for the best, won't it, Mother?"

"It will work out, Jane," Louise said quietly from her chair. "It will all work out."

* * *

Adam Gentry's appetite had not returned but he was consciously eating his meals knowing that the last few months had made him thinner, and weaker, too, as he substituted whiskey for real food. He'd worked all day in the barns with George, the Paradise stable master, as he'd done all week in preparation for the foaling that would be coming soon, and his arms and shoulders felt it. With eleven foals to be born, everyone would have to be fit and able, including him.

Dinner was nearly done, and he was ready to immediately retire to his rooms as he'd been doing for the last few weeks that he hadn't been drinking any alcohol. He wondered if he would ever be able to indulge his love of wine again or if he'd forever ruined himself. He didn't want to be like old Pete, who hung around the stables in Winchester, mucking stalls, carrying wood, or doing whatever would earn him a penny or two to spend at the tavern on watered-down rye or even beer. He'd just put his hands on the arms of the chair he sat in at the head of the table, ready to kiss his mother on the cheek and bid everyone a good evening, when Jim Somerset spoke up.

"I have something to tell you," Jim said and cleared his throat. "I wish Matt and Annie were here, so I wouldn't have to repeat it."

Adam lowered himself back into his chair. Jim was looking at his dinner plate, distracted and pale. Olivia was watching him, staring at him somberly. Her face was lined with worry. His mother was leaning forward in her seat and staring at Jim, concern in her eyes. When Jenny came in to clear dishes, Eleanor shook her head and then rose to close the dining room doors.

"What is it, Jim? We are all family here," Eleanor said to him and reseated herself.

Adam felt a frisson of apprehension or dread that had his palms sweating: that there was some impending dilemma or drastic change that he would be unable to solve or fix and that had put his normally even-keeled brother-in-law into the state he was in. And now that he thought about it, Jim and Olivia hadn't been as starry-eyed and giddy with each other as they usually were of late. He'd overheard his mother asking Olivia a few days before if there was something the matter, but his sister had shaken her head and changed the subject. For himself, he would admit that he was just rejoining the living as it were, barely enough to notice someone else's pain and not be completely blinded by his own.

"We *are* family here and that's why we wanted to tell you something before you heard it from others," Olivia said, not taking her eyes from her husband.

Jim licked his lips and stared at the table's centerpiece. "My sister Emmaline is expecting a child."

Eleanor tilted her head. "Emmaline is?"

"Yes."

"Well, that is very wonderful news," Eleanor said, never taking her eyes from Jim. "How is she feeling?"

"Mother! I'm not sure we can call it wonderful news," Olivia said. "Emmaline is devastated and her family, Jim's family, mine, too, are concerned for her."

"*Devastated* is a strong word," Eleanor said.

"Mrs. Gentry," Jim said quietly. "She's not married."

"She is not," his mother said. "But the birth of a child is always a blessing, and she's certainly not the first woman to have found herself in this situation."

"Emmaline?" Adam said. "Emmaline is expecting?"

"Yes, Adam," Olivia said, allowing some exasperation to color her words. "Emmaline is expecting."

"Jim. Who's the father?" he asked.

Jim looked at him directly. "I don't know, and she won't say, although I think Nettie has an idea." He stood suddenly, pushing his seat back as he stood and making it rock on its back legs until it dropped with a thud. "She won't tell me"—he ran a hand through his hair—"I want to kill him! Whoever he is!"

Adam, Eleanor, and Olivia were all staring at this giant of a man, ordinarily as gentle as a man could be, red-faced and angry and itching to break something.

"Jim," Olivia whispered.

"I am taking a walk," he said. They heard a bang as the front door slammed.

"Mrs. Somerset must be very upset," Eleanor said. "I didn't mean to sound flippant, Olivia. I understand it is a dire situation for a young woman. Fortunately, Emmaline has family and friends to support her, but this will surely be a test of her mettle and fortitude. There will be talk."

Olivia nodded. "Jim and Emmaline are particularly close. He's very upset as you could see. We're considering adding on an addition to our house while it's still being built to include a small apartment where Emmaline could live with her baby, similar to the rooms Matt and Annie had for Ben while he lived with them before he passed on, although she's talking of moving in with her father's aunt in New York where she could say that she is a widow."

"Ah. I hate to see her go so far away," Eleanor said.

"It is so unfair." Olivia blew out a breath. "She's not the only person responsible for this child, but she will bear all the burden."

"But there will be a child and there can be no happier moment for any woman," Eleanor said. "We can be concerned *and* joyous for her."

Olivia looked at her mother. "You are right, I suppose. I've been concentrating entirely on the negative and have failed to see that I will have a new niece or nephew outside of Matt and Annie's Teddy and Ruth, and Jim's sister Nettie's children."

Eleanor smiled. "Why don't you stop down to see Matthew and Annie tomorrow, and Teddy and Ruth, too, of course. They always brighten your day. Perhaps Matthew can talk to Jim alone while you speak to Annie."

"Knowing Matthew, he'll want to kill someone, too," Olivia

said. "But he may be able to calm Jim down. He hasn't slept for a week since we found out."

Adam kissed his mother and sister and went upstairs to his rooms. He undressed and put on a pair of drawstring pants that were soft with washings and a thick robe. He sat down in his chair beside the windows of his room that overlooked the woods. He pulled the footstool up close to his chair and propped his legs on it. He stared out into the darkened landscape as the sun set. Leaf buds were just beginning to be noticeable, and he'd seen deer frolicking in the woods that very morning. Spring was near. Foals would be birthed, and the cycle of life would begin again.

He pictured Emmaline and could hear her sharp wit. She was not a smiling, giggling girl, but she was essentially a happy one, he believed. He doubted she would ever marry or be satisfied to live out her life with her mother. Emmaline did not suffer fools and he imagined the choices for a beau or a husband in Winchester were slim for a woman like her. Perhaps there was a solution, though.

CHAPTER 3

"What do you think, George?" Adam asked as he stood with the stable master in the wide aisle in the middle of one of the Paradise barns. He smelled the familiar hay and manure and horse surrounding him in the stalls holding the expectant mares and was glad to be there, clear headed and cognizant of the sights, sounds, and energy of the stables. That awareness had been muted by grief and liquor for months, until today it seemed.

"I think Diamond will be the first to drop, Mr. Gentry."

"I agree. Let's hope these births are spread over a few weeks. It will be very busy here regardless of when they come, though."

George nodded. "It will." He looked up and down at Adam in his dark suit. "I'm thinking you won't be working out here today but I'm very grateful for the time you've spent here lately. I needed your guidance."

Adam shook his head. "Not my guidance, George. You just needed someone as familiar with this stable as you are to listen to you and work out issues with."

"No one has your instincts." George shook his head. "Your brother and sister and mother know the stables, but they don't make decisions the same as you. You know what to do and how to do it. I'm grateful to have you here. We've missed you."

"Thank you," he said.

Sometimes it felt as if no one would notice his absence if he were gone. And although it was nice to hear George say those words, it wasn't quite the same as if a singular person missed him. A singular female person that needed him. Olivia had Jim, and Matt had Annie. Mother had her memories and the house. He missed Josephine with an ache, but she was gone, and he thought what he was about to do would ensure that someone would need him. That someone might miss him.

One of the stablemen saddled York for him and he rode out, headed toward the town of Winchester. He hadn't been completely sure that what he was doing was the right thing, but the more he thought about it, the more he was certain he *was* making the right decision. He wasn't a Gentry for nothing, after all. He didn't see his mother standing in the window of the main room of the house, watching him ride away in his Sunday clothes.

* * *

"EMMALINE? MAY I COME IN?"

"Yes, Mother," she said and stood from the rocking chair by the window of her bedroom. Betsy had moved in with Jane and now Emmaline had this room all to herself, as she'd always craved even though she and Betsy were close. She wondered if her mother was concerned she'd taint Betsy before she could get her younger sister to the altar and married. But Emmaline had been sewing, of all things, and would have preferred to parade through town with every eye on her rather than stitch the ridiculous blankets that her mother had forced her to begin. She'd talk to anyone, even her youngest brother, Phillip, if it meant she didn't have to ply this needle one moment longer.

"Emmaline, dear, you have a visitor," her mother said while wringing her hands and not quite meeting her daughter's eyes.

"A visitor? Tell them to go away. I'm not a circus animal."

"It's Adam Gentry, dear. Jim's brother-in-law. Olivia's brother," she said with a weak smile.

"I understand how family relationships work, Mother. Tell him I am ill. Tell him whatever you want to tell him. I am not coming downstairs."

"I've already told him you're under the weather. He asked me to please beg you for a moment of your time. I think he knows, Emmaline."

"Of course, he knows. Jim and Olivia wouldn't wait and let Mrs. Gentry and Adam find out at the mercantile. Of course, he knows. I have nothing to say to him and I have to get back to my sewing."

Emmaline plopped down in the rocker and watched as her door closed slowly. She was putting her mother in an awkward position, she knew, but she really didn't want to talk to anyone outside of her small family sphere. Even then she'd rather talk to Betsy than any of them. She knew eventually she was going to have to leave her room, join life again, but she didn't have to do it quite yet and it would be much easier to do when she moved to Aunt Madge's. There she could be Emmaline Smith, widow. She was seriously considering Jim and Olivia's offer to add on an addition to their house for her, though. She adored Jim and had always liked Olivia well enough and knew that Olivia made her brother very, very happy. It would be hard to take the stares if she remained in town, but it wouldn't be—

Her bedroom door opened, and her mother poked her head inside.

"Mother, please," she began but stopped speaking as the door opened wide and Adam Gentry walked into her room.

"I know this is unusual, Mrs. Somerset, but certainly you've known me and my family long enough to know that I intend nothing untoward. But I would like to speak to your daughter alone."

Adam stared at her as he spoke to her mother and she could see Jane and Betsy behind him, eyes wide and their hands over their mouths.

"It's not p-proper, Adam," her mother stuttered.

"I'm fine, Mother. Stand outside my door if you wish."

Emmaline looked at him and noticed that he was thinner than the last time she saw him. He was still very handsome and even intimidating, filling the room with his presence. He was the oldest among her generation of Gentrys and Somersets but had been removed a bit from the rest of them as they grew up together. A bit apart from John and Matthew and Jim, who'd been fast friends growing up, and from Olivia and Nettie and Marabelle Winston, whose family owned the mercantile, and her. He hadn't been aloof, but he hadn't gotten into the same type of trouble that John and Matthew had. Women swooned over him, and he smiled back and tipped his hat in such a way that made a female feel as if she was the only person of her sex in the world. Except right now he wasn't looking so sure of himself and not particularly happy, either.

She'd always liked him up until a minute ago when he walked into her bedroom. She didn't even try and hide the bulge in her skirts.

She waited until the door clicked shut. "Can I help you with something, Adam?"

He nodded and put his hat on her dresser. He picked up a ladder-back chair from the corner and looked at her. "May I?"

She shrugged and watched him put the chair down not three feet away from her chair. He sat down and looked up at her.

"I understand that you are in a family way."

She didn't say a word, just lifted her eyebrows.

"What are your plans?"

"I'm not sure I want to talk to you about my plans. They are private."

"I can understand that." He nodded then looked down at his hands and back up to her face. "Let me ask you this then. Are your plans, whatever they are, fixed, with no possibility of changing your mind?"

She shrugged. "I don't know. I'm just trying to get through each day. When I must decide for certain, I will do so. Why do you ask?"

"I believe I have a solution for you, if you are amenable."

She laughed bitterly. "A solution? I doubt that sincerely, although I thank you for considering my happiness. I am in the situation I am. There is no changing it." She could feel hot tears welling in her eyes. *Damnation!* She would not embarrass herself with tears and swiped her face with her hands.

He was silent for what seemed like several minutes but must have been much less than that. He was staring at her and smiled, a sad, faraway one although it showed hints of the Adam she knew before.

"I was in love," he said and cleared his throat. "I don't know if Olivia ever said anything about it."

"She did. You have my sincerest sympathies. Olivia said you were devastated. What was her name?"

"Josephine. Her name was Josephine Wright. She was sister to my closest friend when I attended Franklin College before the war."

"Ah, yes. Olivia did tell us that much. When did she pass away?"

"This past November first. Her appendix burst, and she was overcome with infection. Her brother and I were with her the entire time."

"I'm terribly sorry, Adam. It wasn't public knowledge and we didn't quite know how to give you our sympathies. My family, I mean. But you have them. My sincerest sympathies."

"Thank you. We would have married by now if she had lived, I'm certain of it."

Emmaline leaned forward and touched his hand where it rested on his knee. "I'm sure you would have. You've been widowed without the benefit of marriage."

Adam brought his head up abruptly and nodded. "Yes. That is quite true. I've never thought of it that way, but it is true."

The door to her room opened. "Emmaline, dear. Is everything all right?"

She shook her head. "Adam tried to ravish me, but I pushed him out my window. Yes, Mother. We're fine. We're just talking. This is Olivia's older brother!"

The door closed, and she could hear Jane asking what *ravish* meant. Adam's shoulders shook, and he looked up at her ruefully. "I would never allow myself to be pushed out the window."

She laughed as if she had not a care in the world and so did he. She looked at him closely. "Why have you come, Adam?"

He stood abruptly, right in front of her and she went to stand, too, but he knelt down on one knee before she could move. She shook her head and backed up in her chair.

"What are doing, Adam? Sit down, please."

His face was close to hers and she could see the gold flecks in his green eyes. She smelled mint, maybe a cologne or his tooth powder. He was wearing a black suit of fine fabric, a starched white shirt, a red silk tie, and a red and grey plaid vest. He looked like a picture out of a book. Romantic and full of love.

He picked up her hand from where it lay on her lap and looked into her eyes. "Emmaline Somerset. Will you marry me?"

The air left the room. She couldn't breathe. Had he said what she thought he'd said?

"Pardon. I thought you asked me . . ."

"I did, Emmaline. Will you be my wife?"

"Adam. I am expecting a child. You are older than me. We

hardly know each other." Everything going through her mind was coming out of her mouth it seemed.

"I know you're expecting a child. I will be that child's father, unless of course, you intend to have a relationship with the father."

She shook her head, feeling dizzy. "No. Never. I'll never."

"Then I will be the father from the day of our marriage on. That child will be my child."

Tears spilled down her cheeks. He was sincere, she was certain of it, and anyway, this was Adam Gentry, a trustworthy man if there ever was one.

"I am ten years older than you if my math is correct. But still not that old," he said and smiled. "Not an old man quite yet."

Something tugged at her heart. He wasn't certain of himself. Adam Gentry wasn't completely sure how this would end, and he must have known it could be embarrassing, mortifying really, if it were to get out that an expectant twenty-two-year-old with no prospects for marriage had turned him down. It was most endearing. But there were other reasons.

"We don't know each other very well, but successful marriages have begun on less. I believe we respect each other and each other's families. My parents married after only knowing each other for a few days. You know the story. She was the love of his life and he hers," he said.

"How," she whispered and stopped to gather her senses and wipe her face, "how can you respect me? I had relations with a man I'm not married to. How can you enter a marriage if you don't at least respect your wife?" She could not look him in the eye.

He turned her face to him with one finger under her chin. "Emmaline"—he shook his head—"whatever the reasoning or circumstances that led to your state, it was a small piece, just a sliver of your life, that I know you have always lived well. You have always loved your family and served them. Why ever would I judge a lifetime on one instance, on one episode?"

His words choked her and made her eyes fill again with tears. Made her believe that there were sensible persons still to be found. She couldn't trust her voice for a full minute. "You do not love me. You would be rescuing me but what is in it for you?"

He stood and sat back on his chair. "We will suit each other, I think. I wish to have children and to do so I must marry. We will be kind to each other. I'll not lie to you, though. I don't believe I'll ever love anyone in that way again. I don't have it to give you or anyone else. But you will have my name, my protection, and you will have my honor, which is all I have left to give."

Emmaline sat back on her chair and stared at him. Was it possible that he was going to save her from what would be an uncomfortable and no doubt lonely life? Was it possible she was considering this wild idea? Of course, she was. She'd known him all of her life. This was Adam Gentry. Handsome, wealthy, maybe broken, but so was she in some ways. Would it be enough for a lifetime? Would she give up all the other possibilities for her life that she'd lain in bed at night and dreamed of? But hadn't she already given them up that night in Brunsville?

She looked up at him suddenly and found him staring at her. He wanted children and would expect her to lie with him. She was strangely interested. What would it be like to have sexual relations with him? She'd never in her life thought of him in that way. He was Olivia's oldest brother. She'd looked at his brother, Matthew, and some other men in town and thought about what it would be like to kiss them but never, ever thought that of Adam. But really, what could she possibly be thinking to consider turning him down? She would have security, a father for this child, she would have resources, and she would not be dependent and obligated to those that fed and clothed her. Surely, a role of the husband and wife was to provide for each other. She would have her dignity. She wouldn't be solely an obligation, would she?

She licked her lips and looked at him squarely. "Yes. I will marry you."

He sat back in his chair and smiled a lopsided grin. "Thank you, Emmaline. We will do well together and raise this child and others as a family."

The door opened. "Emmaline. You must tell me what this is about, dear," her mother said.

Emmaline stood. "Adam has proposed marriage to me and I have accepted him."

Betsy and Jane caught their mother as she slumped and just before her head hit the bedroom floor.

"This is rather an inauspicious start. Your mother has fainted," Adam said quietly from behind her.

Emmaline and Jane fanned their mother's face while Betsy ran a cool rag over her wrists. Phillip came into the room and asked quite calmly if she had died. Emmaline looked up at Adam and as serious a face as he was wearing she couldn't help herself but to bark out a laugh. He looked at her and the corner of his mouth hitched.

Louise Somerset woke with a start. "Emmaline. What did you say?"

Adam reached down and helped her up. "I have asked your daughter to marry me and she has consented."

Louise held a hand to her head. "Can we please go downstairs into the parlor? We cannot speak of this in one of the sleeping rooms! Phillip ask Helen to bring coffee and tea in and some of the lemon sponge cakes she made this morning. Oh, dear! Hurry girls," she said as she shooed Jane and Betsy ahead of her.

Emmaline turned to Adam after everyone had left the room. "Are you quite sure? We could end this right now if you're having any misgivings."

* * *

Strangely, Adam had no second thoughts. He felt almost lighthearted, although he had no illusions that they wouldn't face obstacles. He was doing the right thing. Emmaline was the sister of Jim, whom he'd always respected but had begun to view lately as more of a brother and less of an in-law. Jim and Olivia were both fond of Emmaline and had both suffered with the news of her pregnancy. He could provide peace to both families at little cost to himself.

"I'm not having any misgivings," he said. "I'm going to go home now and leave the details to you and your sisters and mother. I will be back at four, if that is convenient, to take you to Paradise so that you can dine with us."

"There is no need for you to return," she said. "I can walk that short distance."

Adam shook his head. "We are engaged to be married and you are expecting our child. I'll bring the gig and escort you."

"Oh," she said. "Very well. I'll be ready."

Adam had anticipated feeling that while this marriage was not the end of his life, it would be the acceptance that he would not soar in any conceivable way, that a quiet middle ground would be found with some contentment and caring on both of their sides. But that was not how he was feeling. He was feeling rather excited to tell his family, but with that thought came a vision of Josephine. Guilt followed, heavy on his shoulders and in his heart. But she would not want him to live a life alone and bereft of all the comforts of family. She had loved him, and he her.

He would not allow his grief and, with an impending marriage to a woman other than Josephine, guilt, to keep him from some happiness, though. He mustn't, or he may as well find that pistol and end it all. His life would change very little after he married but he would have a companion. She would do whatever his mother did, and he would continue to manage the stables and the growing number of investments he'd made on behalf of the family. She would raise their children and they would console each other in their old age. He would be as happy as he could be and intended to start at that moment looking forward to this union. He kicked York to a run and handed him off to a stable hand after riding up the Paradise drive.

He went in the house immediately and saw their housekeeper. "Jenny, do you know where mother is?"

"Yes, Mr. Adam. She's in her rooms with Miss Olivia choosing paint colors for your sister's new house."

"Would you ask them to join me in the main room in a few minutes? Is my brother-in-law here?" He turned. "What is Mabel preparing for dinner? I've asked Matt and Annie to join us and I'll have a guest, too. Can you see if we have any champagne?"

Jenny smiled. "I'll get your sister and your mother in just a moment and check with Mabel about tonight's menu."

"Don't forget the champagne."

"I won't," she said and turned to the door. "And here is Mr. Somerset."

"Is there something wrong?" Jim asked as he pulled off his jacket and looked at Adam.

"Not at all. I have some news I'd like to share with you. Will you come into the main room?"

It occurred to Adam on the ride that he needed to speak to Jim first as the head of the Somerset family. Emmaline had said yes but there were courtesies to observe, and this was Jim. Olivia's husband. The man who'd been hauling his drunken ass to bed for several months. Jim sat down and looked up. Adam sat down across from him. He smiled.

"I've asked Emmaline to marry me and she's said yes. I suppose I should have spoken to you first, but I didn't want Emmaline to feel any undue expectations or obligations, as you are my brother-in-law. We'll be married soon, I think. She's coming here for dinner tonight."

"Did you say you've asked Emmaline to marry you?"

Adam nodded. "I have, and she has honored me with her hand."

Jim stood and wandered to the windows overlooking the stables. There were several long minutes of silence that had Adam in sympathy with his sister about her husband's quiet nature. But he turned then.

"You mean to marry her so that she will not have this child alone. So that she and my mother will not be embarrassed. It's a fine sacrifice to make and one that ensures her future." Jim studied him. "The drive to be virtuous, to be heroic, can be a powerful thing and you're not feeling whole yet. Will this sacrifice bring you misery, and with it, unhappiness for Emmaline?"

"You act as though your sister doesn't deserve a marriage. Would you rather her be alone with a child and a reputation that she doesn't deserve?"

Jim shook his head. "No. If anyone deserves happiness, it's Emmaline. But she is . . . she is different."

"We're all different," he said. "I believe that Emmaline and I will get along. I think we'll be good partners, and isn't that what marriage is all about?"

"This situation has changed her, has diminished her, in her own eyes, I believe. I've known for months that something wasn't right for her, but I had no idea what it was. If she recovers herself after this child is born, she will challenge you in every conceivable way. She doesn't suffer fools and will talk about nearly any subject and give her opinion." He stared at Adam. "I will not tolerate her unhappiness. I would gladly insert myself between you and her even if it is not legal or right in the eyes of the law or the church and could cause discord between our families. She isn't an object to be pitied."

"I didn't make you suffer through a lecture such as this when you were dallying with Olivia," he said and arched a brow. "I've known you all of my life and knew that you were an honorable man, albeit a stupid one, when it came to her. Are you implying that I would conduct myself in a dishonorable way? That I would be a tyrant? A bully?"

"I don't believe so," Jim said evenly. "I believe you will act the gentleman because you are one. But I also believe that you're doing this because you perceive you can fix this, whereas you'll never bring Miss Wright back from the dead."

Adam crossed the room in a few quick steps and got within inches of Jim's face and snarled. "Do not attempt to diagnose me. I have made an honorable offer of marriage to your sister and I believe you should be happy for the both of us. And don't ever, ever speak my Josephine's . . ."

Jim stared at him until he looked away. Adam took a deep breath. *My Josephine?* She was dead and gone from all of this earth except perhaps from his heart and mind. Emmaline could never replace her but that didn't mean he couldn't be a good husband to her. He looked up at Jim and spoke quietly.

"I've discussed the fact that I am not in a position to offer love to her nor will I ever be. I told her, and I will tell you, I offer my protection, my name, and my honor. She understands what I am capable of. I intend to care for her and all of our children, including the one she carries now. She will be well looked after."

Jim smiled a bit then. "I'm sure you'll do as you say. It remains to be seen if Emmaline allows it."

Adam stepped back as the door to the main room opened and his mother and sister stepped inside. Olivia went to her husband and flashed Adam a curious look.

"I hear you have invited Matt and Annie and the children for dinner and that you will have a guest, too," Eleanor said and walked up to him, looking at him with her beatific smile and her warm and loving eyes. "How wonderful, Adam."

"You've invited someone to dinner?" Olivia asked.

"I have. Will you sit with me for a moment? Mother? Livie?"

He seated himself across from them and leaned forward, his

forearms resting on his legs. "I have asked Emmaline Somerset to marry me and she has accepted. She'll be joining us for dinner."

His mother jumped from her seat, and he rose. She looked at him with glistening eyes and hugged him and kissed his cheek. She held him tightly and whispered, "You are every bit the man that your father intended you to be and more. I could not be more proud of you." She turned to Olivia and Jim and smiled. "What a joyous day! We will have a new family member and I will have a new grandchild to spoil!"

Livie was staring at him, her hands over her mouth, tears in her eyes. "Oh Adam! Adam!" She launched herself at him, "I've been so worried about her and so worried about you. Is this the right thing for both of you? You know I love you dearly."

He held her close to him and kissed the top of her head. "I believe it's the right thing. I think we'll suit very well."

Olivia started to say something and stopped. She kissed his cheek instead and turned to her husband. "And what were you two discussing when mother and I came into the room?"

Jim cleared his throat and stared at him. "I was congratulating your brother. He's a good and honorable man. My sister is fortunate, and so is Adam."

"That's not exactly what you were saying but close enough," Adam said and stared back. He turned to Olivia. "I've got to get back to town. I told Emmaline I'd pick her up at four. I thought we could gather together, just our family, before Mrs. Somerset and Mother plan something more extravagant."

CHAPTER 4

"I will not, and I am saying this for the last time, I will not have a double wedding with Betsy and Edwin."

"But it would be so lovely," Louise Somerset said to her daughters.

"I have to agree with Emmaline, Mother," Nettie said. "Betsy wants something elaborate and wants some time to plan and I don't think that would suit Emmaline."

Emmaline looked at her mother. "Even if I wasn't expecting a child, and was marrying just because, well, I can't fathom any good reason right now, I wouldn't want ribbons and bows and fuss and all the whatnot."

"What do you mean there's no good reason to marry?" Louise said. "Of course, there is good reason. Every woman wants love, and children, and a family to raise and comfort her when she is old. Why else would you be marrying Adam?"

All of her sisters were looking down at their hands, even Jane, who often mended fences among the family. Emmaline was not. She was staring at her mother and wondering how she'd been born of this woman. "Mother. I am having a baby. I'm unmarried.

That is the only reason that Adam asked and the only reason I said yes."

"Must you take all of the romance and hope out of this?" her mother asked, red-faced, as she twisted her handkerchief.

"There is no romance. Adam is still grieving over the loss of a woman he loved, and I am an unmarried pregnant woman from a family he is related to and has known all of his life who he can offer help to. Don't make this to be something it's not."

"But it could be," her mother said and dabbed her eyes. "Jane. You should not be here listening to all of this talk."

"Jennifer Wyland is going to be married this summer. She's the same age as me," Jane said.

"You are far too young to be thinking about marriage," Louise said.

"I'm not thinking about marriage, but I am not too young to hear about it, do you think, Mother? I understand it's a serious subject," Jane pleaded.

"As far as romance goes, you have managed to land the most elusive and charismatic and *handsome* man in Winchester. Think about it," Nettie said and made a disgusted face. "What if he was some spindly, balding man missing his teeth." She shivered.

"Nettie! A person's looks do not make his character. Adam Gentry is a gentleman through and through regardless of his looks or lack of them," their mother said.

"Well, I say it's better to crawl in bed every night of your life with Adam instead of Jerimiah Finch."

Jane blushed, Betsy laughed, and their mother shouted her reprimand even as she walked out of the room and declared her head was pounding so much that she must lie down. Jane hurried after her mother and offered to brew some willow bark tea to help her relax. Nettie and Betsy followed Emmaline to her room while she changed her dress to go to the Gentry's for dinner.

"What did he say, Emmaline?" Nettie said as soon as she closed the door on Emmaline's bedroom.

Emmaline shrugged and pulled her dress over her head. "He told me about the woman he was going to marry, that he loved, and then he just asked me."

"That was all he said? Nothing else?" Betsy asked.

"He said he could never love me but that he wants children and needs to marry to have them."

Nettie sat down on the bed. "Do you want to marry him? Have his children?"

Emmaline plopped down onto the stool in front of her vanity and looked at herself in the mirror. "I suppose," she said. "But I can't think of that or anything that comes after that until this child is born."

"John and I made love up until my eighth month with both children. John asked the doctor and he said it was fine. I can't believe he asked him, though. I would have been mortified. What?" she said to the shocked faces of her sisters.

"I don't want to know about this! Good Lord! Why would you tell us?" Emmaline asked.

Nettie shrugged. "It's part of marriage. You're both going to be married soon. It's not like you won't be having relations with Edwin, Betsy. I've seen how you look at him."

Betsy blushed "When he kisses me, I can hardly think straight," she said and then whispered, "And then I think about taking my clothes off. Am I terribly wicked? Am I going to Hades?"

Nettie laughed. "Of course, you're not going to Hades! There would be no children on this earth if women did not take off at least some part of their clothing. Has mother told you what is going to happen?"

"I didn't quite understand what she meant."

"Did she talk about noodles?" Nettie asked, and Betsy nodded. "Thank God John explained the particulars to me before we married." She looked out the window and sighed. "Hearing him talk about it was quite invigorating."

"Edwin stutters so when he asks to kiss me that I hate to pepper him with questions," Betsy said.

Nettie sat up on the bed. "Lock the door, Betsy. Here's the thing. Mother's description isn't quite right. You know boys have something between their legs."

Betsy gulped. "Yes. I mean I remember bathing Phillip."

"John said that all men have different sizes of them, just like women have different size bosoms. When a man gets aroused because you're kissing or he's touching you or you're touching him, his," Nettie said and swirled her hand below her waist, "gets large and stiff and it goes between your legs and inside you. That is how a baby is made. At least now one of you will know what to do, Betsy."

"It's called a penis, Nettie," Emmaline said as she brushed her hair.

"I'm going to die," Betsy said. "That is a dreadful word."

"Where did you hear that word, Emmaline?" Nettie asked.

She shrugged. "Jim has some books, scientific ones and ones from the Far East that talk about it. There are even pictures."

"Jim?" Betsy gasped.

"Where are they?" Nettie asked.

"They were in his rooms behind the forge in a locked trunk under his bed, but they're gone. He must have taken them to Paradise when he and Olivia married."

"What happened?" Nettie asked.

"I was changing the sheets on his bed and saw the trunk. He must have forgot to lock it because every other time I was alone in his room it was locked."

"I don't mean the books, Emmaline," Nettie whispered. "I mean what happened in Brunsville?"

The room was completely silent other than the patter of Emmaline's heart in her ears. She stared at her hands and thought back to that night and to the man, no, that boy who'd planted this child in her. He'd been clever and funny and had danced with her twice. What a fool she was!

"Was it that Henry person? Carter's cousin?" Nettie asked.

She turned in her seat. "I'm not going to talk about it. Ever. So, there is no use asking me."

"It's just that I feel so guilty," Nettie said and swiped her hand across her eyes. "You were with John and I that night. After you told us that you were expecting, John wanted to get Jim and Matt and ride to Brunsville and . . . I've barely been able to keep him from sharing his suspicions with them."

"We are not going to discuss this, and you have no reason to feel guilty. In any case, Adam has said from the moment of our marriage this child will be his. There'll be no more questions because he or she is Adam's and my child."

"He said that?" Betsy asked.

"He did. Without hesitation."

"He is a romantic, then, even if you are not." Nettie walked over to the dressing table to drop a kiss on her sister's head. "Come along, Betsy. Emmaline needs to get dressed."

* * *

"Did you decide anything about a wedding date or details?" Adam asked as they rode to Paradise in the Gentry gig.

She shook her head. "My sister Betsy recently became engaged to Edwin Crawper. My mother wants us to have a double wedding with them. I told her we were not going to do that."

"Olivia mentioned their engagement. I can't say I'm sorry you decided against a double wedding. I already feel like an old man, and your sister is younger than you yet and I don't think Edwin Crawper is much older."

"I'd prefer we had the ceremony at home or at Paradise with just our families. What would you like to do?" she asked.

"Whatever suits you is fine with me, but I don't want anyone to get the idea that there is any shame in this marriage because there isn't. I don't want anyone thinking we're hiding away."

Emmaline looked at his profile. His hat was pushed back on his head and his hair hung in curls around his neck. He still had on the same clothes as when he'd proposed. His face was shadowed with a dark beard. Adam Gentry would be concerned with what others thought but then he was marrying a woman carrying another man's child. He couldn't be *that* concerned. He turned to her then.

"Although in a town this small, folks are going to speculate and guess and gossip. We're not going to pay any attention to them. But I was thinking we'd set the date for next Saturday. Olivia said that your sister is marrying in May and it would be good if there was any talk it had died down by then. We don't want to overshadow her wedding with questions or comments."

"*If* there is any talk?" she asked and took a deep breath.

He *harrumphed*. "Did you and your sisters and mother decide on anything else? A dress for you? Flowers? Did you talk about any of that?"

They were pulling up outside the Gentry home and Emmaline thought about seeing Olivia and Jim, Jim especially, and talking to Mrs. Gentry, and Matt and his wife. She liked the Gentrys, all of them, but she wasn't quite sure how she'd fit in. She never fit in at home, she thought to herself, why would she fit in here?

"We talked about penises actually," she said.

He turned to her with a start as he pulled the horse to stop. A young boy came up from the stables and took the reins from his hand. Adam closed his mouth and climbed down, coming around the gig to help her down.

"I'm sorry. What did you say? I don't think I heard you," he said.

She put her hand in his and stepped down to the ground. Emmaline looked up at him. "We talked about penises." She saw Mrs. Gentry in the doorway. "Best get this over with."

"Mrs. Gentry," Emmaline said and put out her hand after she went up the slate walkway. She didn't know whether to laugh, or cry, or hurry home and curl up in a ball under her covers. It was one thing to say yes to Adam in the privacy of her bedroom. This public reckoning would be much more difficult she imagined, and she couldn't begin to guess his family's reaction.

"Emmaline, dear! Please call me Eleanor or mother if you'd like. Annie does, but then her mother has passed on to her reward and your mother is still near and dear to you." She pulled Emmaline in for a swaying hug and a soft kiss on the cheek.

Emmaline held her arms at her sides, but eventually patted Mrs. Gentry's back. "I'll call you Eleanor, then," she said as they stepped apart.

The woman slipped an arm through hers to guide her inside as if she'd not been to Paradise many times before. "How are you feeling, Emmaline? Would you like to lie down before dinner? I won't have Adam overtax you."

"I'll be fine, ma'am."

"Here is the bride!" Eleanor said then when they walked into the large room that was the original part of the house when she and Mr. Gentry were first married.

The first face she saw was her brother Jim's. He was the tallest person, the biggest person, and he was standing a bit apart from everyone else near the window. She imagined he'd watched Adam hand her down from the gig and follow her inside. It took every bit of her discipline to not run to him and let him hold her and carry her home. He'd been her rock since she was a child and the head of the family since her father's death. He would save her. But did she need saving?

Annie hugged her and held her hands. "I've told Teddy and Ruth that they have a new aunt. They're very excited, although Teddy doesn't want you to take his uncle Adam away," she said smiling.

"I've no intentions of taking him anywhere," she said, and Annie chuckled.

Olivia pulled her away and hugged her tightly. "Everything will work out for the best. Adam is such a fine man, but of course, he is my brother and I'm overly partial. But I think perhaps you two were meant to be together."

"I think we're going to be together because I'm expecting a child and not married, and he is mourning a woman he loved."

The room went silent for a moment with some awkward shuffling of feet and forced smiles all around. She'd been quiet for the last three months or so since she'd known for certain that she was with child, struck dumb perhaps, in the biblical sense, but she'd found her voice, the one that her mother said was the reason she wasn't often asked to step out with a young man or join a group of women in some pursuit, other than Olivia and Nettie and Marabelle. But then why gloss over the truth?

Adam walked to her. He picked up her hand from her side and held it. "Very true, Emmaline. But that doesn't mean we're not going to have a long and happy life together. I believe we will."

She swallowed, knowing she'd made everyone in the room feel uncomfortable and deflated. She didn't mean to. She really didn't. He was looking at her kindly even though she'd said *penis* in front of him and described their upcoming marriage in the rawest terms possible. He'd told her, though, he didn't judge her *for just a sliver of her life*. She felt the damnable tears again.

"I'm going to believe it, too."

Eleanor sighed and pulled Olivia and Annie close to her. "How dear they are."

Matt came forward and broke up the tenseness she was feeling. He picked her up off of her feet and swung her around. "Emmaline! My childhood nemesis and now going to be my sister!"

"Put her down, Matt," Annie said. "She may be feeling peaked!"

Emmaline smiled at him as her feet touched the floor and turned, watching Jim walk to her. She let herself be swallowed up in his arms and leaned against him. She closed her eyes and felt the tears again. He kissed the top of her head.

"You're going to be a beautiful bride and a wonderful mother. I wish Daddy were here to see you but I'm sure Mother will fuss over you enough for four people."

"Thank God Betsy is getting married. She'll have something to think about and fuss about other than me."

She could feel the laughter rumbling in his chest.

"I've been hoping you could find yourself again," he whispered then. "You'll survive, and Adam will always do right by you even if he doesn't always get your jokes."

"Will you join us in the dining room? Are you up to it?" Adam asked her as he joined them.

"I am."

After everyone was seated, Emmaline took her time looking around the spacious and well-lit dining room. All the decorations and furniture were understated and elegant, not surprising knowing Eleanor Gentry, with help from Olivia in the last few years, made the household decisions. Certainly, Adam would not expect her to be involved. She could just fade into the wallpaper as she often did at home or hide away in her room with her passions, left to judge others and be as sarcastic, and even as caustic, as she wished.

"Have you and your mother decided on a date for the wedding?" Eleanor asked her.

"Next Saturday, I think," she replied and looked at Adam.

He nodded. "Saturday it is. Have you decided any of the other particulars?"

"We haven't had much of a chance to discuss it. What would you like to do?"

"I'd like to get married at church by Reverend Pendleton if he is able and then have a meal afterwards. What do you think?"

Everyone else at the table began to talk among themselves and it gave an illusion of privacy to her conversation with Adam. "I hate to ask my mother to do a large meal with Betsy's wedding coming up and all the parties and whatnot she and Edwin want to have. Would you mind terribly having a meal here? We could have the wedding here as well, I suppose. No need to go into town."

Adam shook his head. "I'd like to ride through town from the church to here in the carriage. I want to make sure everyone sees how happy we are."

"Oh. You truly don't want to hide."

"No. I don't, and I think you do but I believe it will be best in the end if we begin as we mean to go on. I mean to treat you like the respected and cared for wife you will be."

He was going to force this, it seemed, and maybe he did know best in this particular thing. She'd convinced herself over the last three months that she'd never be social again. That thought was not a hardship but perhaps it was wildly unrealistic.

"And the meal?"

"We will have your family and mine for dinner. We may set up some tables in the ballroom as it might be easier for the staff as there'll be nearly twenty of us with the reverend and his wife. Can you speak to Mabel about the menu you'd like?"

She shook her head. "I've not had any appetite for months. Nothing sounds good to me. Why don't you choose the meal?"

CHAPTER 5

Saturday dawned crisp and cool and damp, but the sun was shining brightly now and was drying off the grasses and the stone patio where Adam now stood. He was not dressed yet for the day in the gray suit he'd chosen to wear. He wanted to relax and clear his mind before he was overwhelmed with how permanent and momentous the occasion was.

It was his wedding day. It was as far away from what he'd anticipated that day would be like as he could possibly imagine. His grief would not magically disappear, he knew that, but he was determined to release Josephine from his heart and mind where he'd clung to memories of her to soothe himself when he felt all was lost. He must at least try or there would be no chance that his marriage to Emmaline would make either of them happy. There was no dull mist of alcohol any longer that could allow him some reprieve from pain. He was glad of that, though. Grief was the sort of thing one had to get through, not avoid, he'd learned, and Josephine's death had proven it to him, although he'd avoided that very thing since the moment she stopped breathing, he realized.

He was going to marry Emmaline Somerset in a few hours. He was glad he could give something to someone to ease their pain or embarrassment and Emmaline was in need of some ease. He'd known her forever as part of the Somerset family, although he knew Nettie and Jim more intimately as they were closer to his age. Now he was to be related to that family even more than when Livie married Jim. He hadn't gotten to know Emmaline much more this week, either, as she'd been feeling poorly on two of the occasions when he'd visited, walking with him just once in the backyard of the Somerset home. Neither of them had shared anything personal, keeping their remarks to the weather and other subjects such as the color of a new shawl that her mother had purchased. *Good God!*

He was hoping to feel a spark of interest in her physically, not that he thought that he couldn't get the work done to bring about the next generation of Gentrys. He could. He could close his eyes and kiss her and envision Josephine. *What a horrible thought to have on this of all days!* He would have to exert some effort and find an attraction between them regardless of how slight, even if it were just the color of her hair or texture of the skin on her hands. She was to be his bride and he owed her that, and it wasn't as if she was unpleasant to look at. He'd just not bothered looking all that much.

It was hard to tell her shape, though, under the brown or gray dresses she wore, that she'd worn as long as he'd known her. And this pregnancy had left her thin with a pallor to her face. She looked sickly. Nothing like what his sister-in-law Annie looked like when she was expecting. She'd looked healthy and robust and feminine and pleased with her circumstances the entire time she'd carried both of her and Matt's children. But he supposed all women were different.

He wondered when Livie would be expecting and was surprised it hadn't occurred in the first year of her and Jim's marriage. It wasn't for a lack of trying, he thought, considering the looks they had for each other or the night he'd wandered by their bedroom past midnight on his way to the kitchen for a glass of milk. He'd been startled by the sound of something hitting a wall with a thud and then their mingled voices talking low, and laughter, and giggles from Livie. He'd felt like a voyeur.

He couldn't quite imagine he and Emmaline being playful and adventurous when they consummated this marriage, even though it would be some months from now. He wouldn't allow himself to envision the sensuous and heated passion there'd been between him and Josephine. But he would do his duty in this marriage and so would Emmaline. What a depressing thought for a day meant to be meaningful and uplifting.

"Hey," he heard from behind him. He turned to see Matt coming toward him with two mugs of something steaming, his feet and his chest bare.

Adam took the cup, blew on its contents, and took a sip. "Thank you. I was up and about before Mabel and didn't want to bother with brewing it."

Matt looked at the trees ahead of them and walked to the stone bench at the edge of the patio. He sat and drank his coffee and sniffed the air.

"You're going to have a nice day. No rain."

Adam *harrumphed*. "You still think you can predict the weather that way?"

"We'll have to see how the weather turns out and then we'll know, I 'spect."

"The weather doesn't matter," he said quietly.

Matt leaned his elbows on his knees and took slow sips of his coffee. "It's not too late, Adam." He looked up.

"What do you mean?" Adam thought he probably knew what his brother was going to say. He was surprised he'd waited this long.

"I mean that if you want to call this thing off, you should do it. You're not in any shape to make a decision like this. Hell, Livie and I wouldn't care if you wanted to give Emmaline money out of the Paradise account to start over somewhere on her own. We both care for her and worry about her, but you don't have to marry her."

"Actually, I do. I've asked her, and she's accepted."

"She's not herself and neither are you."

"And you were completely sane after surviving what you did in Bridgewater and the war? Sometimes we just do the next best right thing in our life. You certainly did when you asked Annie to marry you."

Matt looked down at his hands holding his coffee, and Adam was hoping he'd exhausted that subject. He had not.

"Then wait. What's the rush? Wait until you're both feeling up to this sort of decision."

"What? And let Emmaline face the scorn and the embarrassment alone?"

"It's not your place to save her. She's got a family. She's got people who love her. She's not alone," Matt said and stared at him. "There's a man out there that got her this way, too. Where's he?"

Matt stood when Adam walked to him. "I've chosen to help her. I chose this path. I chose to give her a way out of the mess she found herself in and maybe found a way out of darkness for myself. Let it go, Matt, and don't ever mention the man who got her this way ever again. The baby she's carrying will be mine the moment she says 'I do' and it will be your niece or nephew, too. If you can't do that, don't come around. I mean to make a family of my own."

Matt opened his mouth to continue the conversation but must have thought better of it. He grabbed Adam by the shoulders. "I love you, brother. Whatever you want is what I want for you. I'll be standing right beside you today and be happy to do it."

Thankfully, Matt left him quickly. He was panicked a bit, knowing the truth of what his brother said faced with what honor dictated he do. He took a few long, slow breaths and convinced himself that the future would be good and if it was not, then he must make the best of it somehow.

* * *

ADAM STOOD IN THE FRONT OF THE CHURCH, MATT AT HIS SIDE, his mother, Annie, and Livie together in the first pew holding Teddy and Ruth. He smiled at them, even as his mother dabbed at her eyes with a lace-edged hanky. He looked up and turned toward the doors when Mrs. Pendleton began to play a hymn on the organ at the side of the church.

She was on Jim's arm walking steadily toward him, her hair fixed in a soft bun on the top of her head with a ribbon and a few bluebells adorning it. Her dress was the palest blue, scoop-necked with tight short sleeves and yards of draping silk from under her bosom and over her slightly rounded stomach. She wore lace gloves and held herself erect as a queen. For a moment he forgot all of the reasons that honor dictated to him to save this woman, all the reality of looking to replace Josephine, all the yearning he had to begin a family as he saw Emmaline in a way he'd never seen her before. She was a lovely young woman. Proud and elegant. And she would soon be his wife. There was a spark of interest in her, purely a male reaction, a twitch as it were. He was glad of it and glad to be reaching for her hand as he took it from Jim's.

He smiled at her. Her lips moved, and her eyes darted but then she swallowed and looked him square in the eye. The slightest smile graced her lips, revealing the gap between her two front teeth, and she nodded as if to say let this new story begin. Within no time it seemed, she was his wife. He kissed her cheek and was enveloped from all sides with hugs and kisses and well-wishes.

. . .

SHE WAS MARRIED, EMMALINE THOUGHT TO HERSELF AS SHE settled in beside Adam, twisting the gold band on her finger, in the carriage to go to Paradise for their wedding meal. She'd never had any desire to be married. None at all. She knew there were good reasons to be married but had never matched those reasons to anything she'd ever wanted for herself. But it was too late. She was *married* and had a husband. She looked up sharply at Adam. He was waving and smiling at townsfolk who were out and about, some, she was certain, waiting to see the disgraced bride and the pitiful groom. She'd promised Jim that very morning that she would do her best to be happy and put aside all her other dreams. She just didn't know exactly how to do it.

"Smile, Emmaline," he said and glanced at her. "You're not going to the guillotine."

She let the corners of her mouth tilt up and raised a hand to Marabelle, who was crying and waving her hanky from where she stood in front of the mercantile. "I know that."

He looked at her then and she sucked in a quick breath. He was so very handsome in his gray suit and striped tie. His dark hair had recently been cut and she could smell lemons, maybe from his soap or a cologne. She didn't know, but yet he was her husband.

"You look beautiful, Emmaline," he said and gazed at her, giving her all of his attention even as he urged the horses ahead. "That color suits you and you look like you're feeling better than when I visited on Thursday."

"I am feeling better. Nettie helped me pick out this dress from some ready-made ones over at Bessie's. I've never had much interest in the like but I'm glad I got something new." She looked at him. "It made me feel like I was starting over."

"This is a fresh start for both of us."

You look beautiful. How those words rang over and over in her head, even knowing that beauty was not the essence of a person, not necessary for a soul to be good or evil or even indifferent.

But it was the first time a man had said anything like that to her and it did strange things to her insides. He'd been serious and focused on her when he said it as if she were the center of something for him. Oh, how she wished he'd say it again. She wanted to feel that again. She glanced over at him and found him staring at her. She held his gaze until she couldn't and stared straight ahead instead as the carriage began the descent to Paradise.

THE TABLES WERE SET UP ON ONE END OF THE BALLROOM WHERE the massive marble fireplace was and were covered with pink linen, decorated with delicate embroidered flowers and greenery. The place settings were fine china and cut crystal glassware and silver cutlery. Adam reached for her hand to draw her into conversation with Reverend Pendleton and his wife. He pulled her arm over his and held it steady.

"You look lovely, Emmaline," Mrs. Pendleton gushed. "We are so glad things have worked out so wonderfully for you! The congregation will be thrilled."

She opened her mouth, ready to tell the minister's wife that she couldn't care less about the congregation and if the woman thought she was marrying an old friend of the family because she'd been ignorant enough to let a man under her skirts, then the minister's wife's version of "things working out" was at odds with her own.

"How . . . exceptional," she said instead.

"What a courageous girl you are," Reverend Pendleton said as he nodded kindly.

She could feel Adam's hand tighten around hers and she looked up at him. He wasn't smiling, looked serious in fact, but his eyes were dancing with amusement. She wasn't imagining it. He pursed his lips and kissed the air above her hand where he held it.

"She is *exceptionally courageous*," he said and continued to stare at her, daring her, so it seemed.

Emmaline was nearly overwhelmed with the urge to laugh at the hilarity of his response. She sucked in her cheeks to ward off a nervous guffaw and looked up at Adam. She blinked slowly twice and hoped she looked pitiful enough to make him laugh first. Her mother interrupted, kissing her cheek and laying a hand on Mrs. Pendleton's shoulder.

"Aren't they the most darling couple you have ever seen, Grace?" Louise said as her eyes filled with tears as they'd been almost constantly doing since she'd learned Emmaline was expecting a child. She dabbed them with her ever-present hanky. "The Somerset family is most fortunate, and how I wish Mr. Somerset were here to celebrate with us."

Reverend Pendleton clutched her mother's hand with one hand and Adam's with the other. She and Adam looked at each other at the same time as the reverend offered up a quick prayer.

"I'm going to let my bride rest on the bench in the garden before dinner, Reverend. She's had a tiring day," he said after the amen and led her away from the minister.

They stepped out through the glass-paned double doors that led directly to the stone patio. She leaned back against the cool brick around the corner of the house out of the view of those inside. She clutched her belly with one hand and her mouth with the other. Laughter burst forth through her fingers as her and Adam's eyes met.

He laughed, throwing his head back and then wiping his eyes with the back of his hand. "I don't know what is exceptional about us, but we are."

"We are darling, too," she said as her shoulders shook.

"And courageous. Don't forget courageous."

"Stop. I'm going to have to go to the privy if I laugh anymore and I'll miss dinner."

Her laughter faded suddenly with the reminder of her pregnancy, and she felt a familiar gloom descend that had been trailing her since that night in Brunsville. "It is hilarious, I suppose, because I am none of those things," she whispered. "I'm ordinary and fearful and whatever the opposite of darling is."

Adam straightened and walked directly to her. He looked her in the eye. "Don't. Don't disparage yourself. You are intelligent and witty. You are a lovely woman both inside and out and I was proud to stand beside you today."

"I'm sorry. I'm not usually morose. Nettie said it's normal when expecting to feel excited and happy one moment and terrified and miserable the next," she said. She could get used to his compliments, though, she thought. "I was proud to stand up beside you today, too. You have rescued me, and you are Adam Gentry, the one all the boys envied and the girls flirted with."

"You make me out to be a paragon. I am not. I am not at all."

She looked up at him and told the truth then. "I am glad I married you today. I've been telling myself that I could raise this child alone, that if I lived out my life as a help to my mother as she aged that I would be satisfied. I could do both things and live an adequate life, but it would be lonely. I'm glad I'll have a . . . a partner."

He nodded. "You are very wise, Emmaline Gentry, as well as witty and intelligent and lovely. Let's go inside now and let our families celebrate with us. They are all hoping very much that we are able to make a go of this marriage. We will convince the skeptics."

She swallowed hard. She was no longer Emmaline Somerset. She was Mrs. Adam Gentry. It had not occurred to her once during the preparations for the wedding that her name would change. She was someone she didn't know, a new person. Maybe this *was* her chance to begin again.

. . .

HIS BRIDE WAS EXHAUSTED. SHE ATE VERY LITTLE OF THE FILET of beef or the fresh sole that Mabel had ordered from Baltimore and that had arrived by train, packed in ice and straw. She sipped her water and ate a sliver of wedding cake. The Paradise staff had done a spectacular job on very short notice. Every inch of the house shone from the polish and scrubbing that had been hurriedly completed for his wedding. He must remember to add a bonus to their pay or order a treat of some kind for them. Maybe a perfume or a silk scarf they would never purchase for themselves. Mabel had kissed his cheek before he left for the church, patted his lapels, and told him he was a good man as she knew he would be from the day she met him when he was eleven-years-old.

Teddy, and Nettie and John's children, Rachel and Albert, raced across the slick ballroom floor, twirling and sliding about, and getting terse looks from their mothers. John picked up the three under his arms, the children laughing and wiggling, and took them outside, Matt following carrying Ruth. The Somersets and the Gentrys had two marriages and two successful businesses between them. It was a good alliance, he thought, and reached his arm around his wife's chair, touching her back lightly. He looked at her and realized she was swaying in her seat.

"Emmaline," he said softly. "Would you like to go lie down for a bit?"

"No. I'll be fine."

Adam thought that she really did need some rest as it seemed to him she was holding herself upright by sheer will alone. He stood at his place. Everyone turned their heads to him as if he would be giving another toast like Matt had done, making everyone chuckle, and then Jim, whose wishes for them had everyone in the room misty-eyed, including him. But his mother and Mrs. Somerset, his mother-in-law, strange as that sounded, both looked at Emmaline and stood.

"Come along now," Louise said to Jane and Phillip and Betsy

and motioning to Edwin to help her from her chair. "This has been a long day and I am exhausted."

"Yes. I am as well," Eleanor said. "And these children have near worn themselves out."

Everyone drifted to the front hallway, gathering wraps and kissing children. Jim had Nettie's two in his arms, carrying them outside to their carriage. Adam helped Louise into her seat and kissed her cheek as Edwin gathered the reins and nodded at him.

"See that Emmaline lies down, won't you, Adam? I'm so worried for her," Louise said.

"Of course. It's been a trying week, but I think it was a beautiful and memorable day."

She nodded and looked at him with watery eyes. "It has. Thank you."

Matt and Annie were walking home, and he waved at them after kissing the children and thanking them. He went back inside and found Emmaline hurrying to the door.

"Tell mother to wait," she began and then looked at him, her face going scarlet. "I don't live there anymore, do I?"

He shook his head. "You do not."

Her shoulders slumped, and she weaved a bit where she stood. He swept her up in his arms and headed for the staircase. "It is long past the time that you are napping and giving this baby of ours a rest."

She didn't fight him, and he thought if she had any strength left at all, she would have. Her head rested against his shoulder and she drifted off as he carried her down the long hallway, carefully opening his door and swinging her through straight to his bedroom. He laid her on the bed, and she took a long, slow breath but never opened her eyes. He wasn't sure if he should touch her and just stood dumbly for a few minutes, staring at her. He shook his head and reached down and pulled her shoes off. She moaned, and he smiled thinking he'd like to take his dress shoes off as well. He pulled the pins from her hair and put them on the vanity he'd gotten from the attic and installed in the dressing room beside his bedroom. Her trunk was already open, and he saw several brown and gray dresses hanging up. He found a blanket on the shelf in the dressing room and shook it out over her.

He changed out of his suit, pulled the drapes in the bedroom, and lit a lamp to a soft glow. He found his mother, Jim, and Livie in the main room.

"Is she sleeping?" Eleanor asked.

He nodded. "She was asleep in my arms before I got her to my rooms."

"I've told Mabel and Jenny and Beatrice to take the rest of the evening and tomorrow off," Eleanor said. "They've left a cold tray if anyone is hungry and there is still plenty of wedding cake."

"It's not even six in the evening and I am tired enough that I could sleep for a week," Olivia said.

"Thank you, Livie, and Mother, and you, too, Jim," he said and took a tentative sip of wine. "I know you worked very hard to make this a festive occasion and there are plenty of details I'm sure I wasn't even aware of that you took care of for me and for Emmaline. I think it was for the best, though, considering her sister's upcoming nuptials, to have the wedding quickly."

"There was no use waiting, I agree," Jim said. "I think it was the right thing for Emmaline, even if I did have to ride all over the place picking up flowers and whatnots your mother and mine sent me for."

Adam chuckled. "Better you than me, brother."

Eleanor stood. "I'm for my rooms. I want to stretch out and read a book. Were you able to help Emmaline with her dress?" She looked at Adam.

He colored, feeling silly that he did, and he heard Jim clear his throat. "Ah, no. No, I didn't."

"Come along then, Olivia. We'll get Emmaline into a night-gown, so we don't have to disturb Beatrice or Jenny."

Olivia and Eleanor left the room, and Jim and he looked at each other and quickly looked away.

Adam cleared his throat. "Don't worry, um, about Emmaline, and me. I think it will be best for us to wait to . . . get to know each other better until after our baby is born."

Jim nodded and looked every way except at Adam's face. "Probably for the best."

* * *

ADAM STAYED UP WELL INTO THE EVENING. JIM AND OLIVIA had gone to their rooms long before that and he'd sat looking into the fire in the main room, sipping his wine. He had no desire to drink more than one glass, which he was glad of. He thought long and hard about how to proceed in this marriage—how they could begin getting to know each other. He wasn't thinking about sex, although he had been when he'd shared those awkward sentences with Jim. But he and Emmaline must begin having conversations, thinking about the future, and understanding each of their habits and dreams, and he thought that getting to know each other would only be more awkward, maybe impossible, if they didn't begin soon, as a couple.

He wandered into his room and changed into his drawstring pants and a well-washed undershirt. Emmaline's hair was loose, and she wore a warm-looking nightgown. She was on her side breathing evenly. He sat down on his edge of the bed. This was strange, he thought to himself. There was someone in his bed here and it wasn't Josephine, as he'd expected it would be for some time. He got under the covers, turned on his side, and looked at her. She looked very, very young and very vulnerable. Her eyes fluttered open. For a moment, he saw pure panic in them. She stared at him and pulled the blankets up and around her neck.

"I'm sorry. I was so tired I couldn't stand any longer."

He smiled. "I'm glad you got some rest. You needed it."

"How . . . how did I get in my nightgown?"

"Livie and Mother came up and got you changed. You must have been really exhausted to not realize."

"I was"—she swallowed—"I don't remember changing at all."

"I'm never going to try to hurt or embarrass you, Emmaline. Don't be nervous about that."

"I know," she whispered.

"I do think we're going to have to work at this marriage, maybe more than others have to work at theirs, and I've been doing some thinking about other things as well."

"What other things?"

Adam adjusted the pillow under his head. It was going to be difficult talking about sex to her. It was rarely a comfortable subject, but he and Josephine had been surprisingly open about it. She'd been willing to discuss it matter-of-factly when necessary and sensually all the other times.

It had been a revelation to him, the openness, the erotic nature of language, the intimacy of it all. But this wasn't Josephine. He was thinking that it felt a bit like talking to Livie or his mother about sex, which would have been horrific, but when he glanced at Emmaline and saw her staring at him with wide, dark brown eyes, sleepy and sensual, all the same, with long thick hair a loose riot around her face, and that gap between her teeth, he reconsidered. She was a woman, a desirable one, in his bed, his wife. The woman who would bear his children and be his companion until he was buried in the ground. He felt the stirrings of desire.

"I think it would be wise to wait until after our child is born to have relations," he said and cleared his throat, willing himself to begin as he hoped to go on. "Sexual relations."

She blinked. "I was hoping you thought so. Nettie says that the doctor told John that they could, you know, continue until she was in her eighth month and I know that will be part of our marriage, but I just can't imagine it right now."

"Women talk about that sort of thing, do they?"

"Not all of us but it's near impossible to shut Nettie up. She was telling Betsy about, um, the act, when she mentioned that."

"Your mother didn't tell Betsy?"

"Oh, she did. She told her a story about noodles."

"Noodles?"

"There are dried-up hard ones before the boiling and soft ones after."

Adam felt laughter bubbling up in his chest as he stared at her. And then he laughed until his eyes watered. He couldn't help himself. She was giggling, her shoulders shaking under the blankets.

He finally shook his head. "I'm never going to be able to look at your mother again. Why did you tell me this?" he asked with a smile.

"Some things in life are too hilarious to not laugh at."

"Are you feeling better now?" he asked and reached across to touch her face. "I'm looking forward to this baby, you know that, don't you?"

Her smile fell away. "I can't believe how kind you're being. This baby isn't yours."

"You're wrong about that. This child is my child. I'm very much looking forward to having a son or a daughter."

EMMALINE WATCHED HIM AS HE ROLLED ONTO HIS BACK, adjusting the blankets, with one arm thrown above his head, the very picture of casual masculinity. He didn't close his eyes, just stared at the ceiling. He cleared his throat.

"Josephine was expecting our child when she died," he whispered. "She wasn't very far along."

She pulled herself up on one elbow and leaned toward him. "I am so very sorry. You've had a double loss then. A wife and a child."

He nodded. "I've spent the last six months torturing myself and my family and drinking far too much over it. But I'm done with that." He turned his head to her. "I am married and have a child to look forward to. I am a very fortunate man."

"Olivia never said anything . . ."

"No one knew except Josephine and me. We were going to marry very soon, she wanted something private, just her and I, and then we would tell our families."

The telling was hurting him, she knew, even if his voice hadn't caught, even if he hadn't had to stop to take a breath. She could tell that he was baring his soul to her. He was, ultimately, the courageous one. She admired him for it and laid a hand on his shoulder and patted him as if he were in need of comfort, which she thought he was. His hand came up fast to hold hers down against him. He was taking long, deep breaths and she thought he was fighting tears. He rolled to his side giving her his back and let out a shuddering sigh. Emmaline curled on her side, held her stomach, and closed her eyes.

EMMALINE WOKE UP A WEEK AFTER HER WEDDING FEELING exhausted and as uncomfortable as she had since the beginning of the pregnancy. Everyone told her that within a few weeks she would be full of energy and excited for the coming baby, but that week never came, she really never felt healthy, never felt like doing much more than controlling her rebellious stomach and sleeping. She'd spent most of her first seven days of marriage in bed. Adam was kind, bringing their evening meal to his sitting area, so that she could join him, even in her nightgown a few of those days. But she was determined to get up and join the family for Sunday dinner today.

Adam, Matt, and Jim stood when she went into the dining room. Adam smiled and came to her directly.

"You look as though you're feeling much better, Emmaline," he said and pulled out her chair for her.

"We're so glad you felt up to joining us, dear," Eleanor said. "Adam has been morose without you here."

Olivia smiled. "Do you like stew? Mabel's is delicious, and I know she's made several loaves of fresh bread, too. I can smell it! Although I can't seem to make it correctly, even having watched her make it hundreds of times."

"Are you losing weight now that my sister is cooking for you in your brand-new house?" Matt said with a laugh to Jim.

Olivia raised her brows and Jim winked at her. "We're still getting used to the new stove," he said.

Everyone at the table laughed, even Olivia, whose face was red with embarrassment. "We've been eating at his mother's the nights that my recipes didn't turn out quite right."

"What happened the other nights?" Matt asked.

"We eat at Martha's," Jim said.

Everyone laughed when Jim mentioned the restaurant in Winchester and Emmaline felt better just to be part of it. She hadn't realized how lonely she'd been until then.

"I'm sorry I couldn't help with your move. Adam told me about it, though," Emmaline said to Olivia. "I would like to see it now that's done, though."

Olivia's eyes lit up. "Oh, you must come as soon as you are able. Adam? You must bring her to see our house! I love it, Emmaline. I am so happy." She looked at Jim, who was gazing at her with open adoration.

"I'll bring her as soon as she's up to it," Adam said smoothly with a smile for his sister. "We can discuss it later today."

Mabel served the stew in two large tureens, one for either end of the table. Matt smashed a potato on a plate for Teddy, sitting beside him in a tall chair. Eleanor was tucking a napkin into his little collar and then turned, passing the linen-covered basket of steaming hot bread to Annie on her left. She looked at her family assembled before her.

"I'm so glad you were able to join us today, Emmaline," she said and dabbed her napkin to her mouth. "I have an announcement to make and was hoping I'd be able to say it once and be done with it. Oh, dear, I'm a bit nervous telling you all."

"Mother," Adam said with concern. "Are you well?"

"It's nothing as dreadful as that." She stopped for a moment and laid her silverware down beside her plate. She looked up at them with a smile. "I am moving to Washington to live with a friend I met when Olivia and I attended Josephine's salon."

The table was completely silent until Matthew spoke.

"Did you say you're leaving Paradise, Mother?"

"Who?" Olivia asked.

"What?" Adam said.

"At Josephine's salon, don't you remember, Fiona McKellar? She is a maiden lady and was with her brother, Ian."

"I do," Olivia said. "You're going to live with her? When did this all come about?"

"Miss McKellar and I have been corresponding ever since that evening. She lives alone, her brother still keeps his house he had as a married man even though he has been widowed for some time, and she has stayed all these years in the house where she and her brothers and sisters grew up. She is close to my age and with Aunt Bridget gone now some six months, and a new mistress for Paradise, I think I'd like to do a little traveling and return here for the winter months. I could stay in Aunt Bridget's rooms on the first floor when I come visit, you know, unless you and Emmaline have plans for that area of the house, Adam. Or I could stay with Matt and Annie or Jim and Olivia."

The table was completely silent other than Teddy tapping his spoon on his dish. Emmaline was shocked. She could never imagine her mother moving to another city or traveling with another woman. Eleanor Gentry was everything everyone had always said she was. The strangest thing, though, was when she said Paradise would have a new mistress. She wondered who it would be.

Annie stood and went to Eleanor's side. She bent down and hugged her and kissed her cheek. "How exciting for you! We will always have room for you with us, won't we Matthew. I'll miss you, though. You've been like a . . ."

Eleanor stood and hugged Annie when she began to cry. "I'll miss you, too, and these precious children as well, but I think I've earned some relaxation time now that all of my children are grown and happily settled." She took Annie's cheeks in her palms. "You're as dear to me as Olivia."

Jim cleared his throat and picked up Olivia's hand from her lap where it lay. "When are you planning on going, ma'am?"

"Actually, I leave on the train tomorrow. I've got several trunks packed and ready to go. One of you will have to get me to the station to see that—"

"Tomorrow?" Olivia cried. "Tomorrow? Why so soon? Can you not wait just a little while longer?"

"When Adam announced he was marrying Emmaline, I decided, and wrote to Fiona at that time. These two newlyweds deserve a home of their own to begin their family in. As you all know, Paradise will become Adam's when I pass on, and there was a trust for you, Matthew, and Olivia, to build a home with, which you have both done. This was your father's dream, you know, Adam." She smiled softly at him. "This was the Gentry legacy to his oldest son. It was important to him that Paradise passed down this way."

Emmaline watched Adam swallow. "I don't know what to say, Mother. Other than I wished you'd consulted us before you made this decision."

"I am an adult woman as well as being your mother. I am financially well-situated. I have spent my life caring for Paradise and all its inhabitants, from the moment your father brought me to that single room where it all began all those years ago, not that I would change a thing. It has been the grand work of my life. I loved your father and will continue to love him until I meet him again along with my mother and father and sisters, and Aunt Bridget, too. I have cared for you children and love you all desperately, and that includes, you Annie, and Jim and Emmaline, too. But it is time for me to see some sights and experience some new things and more than that, your wife needs to run her own home, and raise your children, in the way the two of you agree upon, Adam. There is no room for two mistresses. I gladly turn the reins of this household over to Emmaline."

Eleanor smiled benignly and picked up her fork She looked up at her family. "Your dinner is growing cold. Eat, won't you? Mabel will be quite disappointed if you don't."

Mistress? Mistress of Paradise? How absurd! She would have laughed if she hadn't glanced around the table. Adam was concentrating on stirring the meat and potatoes and carrots and turnips in the shallow bowl in front of him. Olivia was close to tears and Jim was trying to calm her. Matthew looked angry and stubborn. She couldn't run a home as large and grand as Paradise and she would tell Adam so as soon as they were alone!

CHAPTER 6

Adam stood with Matt, Jim, Olivia, and Annie on the train platform waving at Eleanor as she waved back through the glass window of the car. She'd been smiling and looking excited the entire morning, even when they'd arrived at the station and Olivia had burst into tears and told her mother as they'd stood there with everyone waiting for the train on the platform with them that she was expecting a child. Eleanor had hugged her close, kissed her forehead, and turned to Jim to kiss him, too, and murmur something in his ear, her eyes shimmering. She would be home to help with both Olivia's and Emmaline's birthing. Matt was looking grim and sad, contrary to his size, and the fact that he was a man grown.

Adam had had a long talk with his mother after dinner when everyone else had gone home. It seemed she'd been thinking about doing this for the last several years. No, she'd never mentioned it to anyone because she didn't want to venture out on her own, but then she and the McKellar woman had become fast friends and she'd thought about buying a home there of her own. Fiona would not hear of it with a ten-bedroom house including a suite of rooms that was to be Eleanor's, a mansion from the sounds of it and well-staffed, in the heart of the city. It seemed to Eleanor that there was some destiny at play.

The five of them stood on the platform as the train chugged away, gradually becoming smaller and smaller in the distance. Olivia was leaning back against Jim, his arms around her. Matt walked to the edge of the platform and kept walking a bit, staring off in the distance at the train as it disappeared, his hands on his hips. Annie walked to him eventually and slid her arm through his.

This change had seemed altogether too much to accept but Adam had spent some time thinking about it after speaking to Emmaline. His wife was terrified at the prospect of managing Paradise, and he was at odds as how to convince her that was exactly what she had to do. He couldn't possibly manage the house and the gardens and the inside staff over the long term when he was already managing the stables and the other businesses that his family had invested in. Granted, she could do nothing until this child was born. But perhaps his mother was correct. Maybe his marriage would never work until they faced the world as a couple, not as an addition to what his father and mother had already built, but rather as their own creation. Eleanor Gentry was stepping out of the way for a new generation of Gentrys to take hold and set their destiny and into her own new future as well.

"So, what do you know about this Fiona McKellar?" he asked Olivia as Matt and Annie returned to them. "There was no opportunity to ask you last night."

"I only spoke with her for a short while, but she was lovely, intelligent, and close to Mother in age. I can see them enjoying themselves thoroughly in the social life in Washington. And her brother, Mr. McKellar, was enamored of Mother, you could tell. Even Josephine mentioned it and she said he wasn't known to escort anyone about except his sister."

"What was he like?" Annie asked. "It would be so nice for a gentleman to pay attention to Eleanor. I think she's a bit lonely, especially with Aunt Bridget gone."

"I don't care if she's lonely or not," Matt said. "And you all know that's not true, but I don't like the idea of a man sniffing around Mother."

"It's strange, isn't it, to think of our mother as anything but a mother." Olivia shook her head, turning to Annie as she did. "Mr. McKellar is tall and well-formed, handsome, too, with a head of thick white hair and kind, pale blue eyes. He was dressed in the latest fashion and made his fortune in bricks and masonry. He was quite attentive as well as another gentleman, a Mr. Hendrix. Mother was the belle of the ball according to Josephine. It was quite lowering for me."

Jim kissed the top of her head. "They all knew to stay away from you."

She tilted her head back and smiled. "There was a handsome one that worked in the State Department, a Mr. Newton, that was looking for an introduction."

"He can look for one all he wants," Jim said. "He's not getting one."

Annie slipped her arm through Adam's as they walked down the steps. "How is Emmaline this morning? She's really had a time of this, hasn't she? When was the last time she saw Dr. Carter?"

"Just a few days before our wedding. He said she should be putting on more weight than she is but that every woman is different. How can she put weight on when she is constantly nauseous?"

"Would you like me to come up to Paradise tomorrow and visit with her, maybe help her get downstairs for a bit?"

"That would be nice if you can spare time from the children."

"Matthew can stay home with them. He leaves the following day to investigate this logging company he wants to invest in or buy. I'm sure he's talked to you about it."

"He has. I think Emmaline would appreciate some company. I'm going to be busy. Foals are starting to drop, and Mabel and Jenny can handle the house, but still it would be good if someone spent some time with her. Maybe I'll ask Livie to come up another day this week."

He helped Annie into their gig and kissed Olivia's cheek and congratulated both she and Jim, not that there was any shock that she was in a family way, before mounting York and turning toward Paradise and his wife.

* * *

EMMALINE WOKE WITH A START AS THE MOONLIGHT POURED IN the window near the bed. She was doubled over and sweating with cramps and aching in her back. She could hear Adam breathing softly on the other side of the bed through the haze of pain.

"Adam," she whispered with all the breath she had. "Adam."

He rolled over and opened one eye and then sat up quickly. "What's wrong, Emmaline? What is it?"

"I don't know!" she cried and let out a moan.

He was out of their bedroom on a run and she could hear him hollering for Jenny to go for George. He was back in their bedroom until he heard George coming down the hallway.

"Go for Dr. Carter, George! Immediately!"

She could hear shouting far away as if she was in a long tunnel of trees that muted sound against their leaves. She could feel a hand touching her face and wiping her brow with a wet cloth. She could hear the worry in Adam's voice as he spoke.

"Emmaline," he said. "Emmaline, can you hear me?"

She licked her lips and nodded, wondering why she wouldn't be able to hear him, even if he did look fuzzy and distant. Pain crashed down on her and she screamed.

* * *

EMMALINE OPENED HER EYES SLOWLY. SHE WASN'T SURE WHERE she was or what time of day it was or if it was nighttime. She could see heavy drapes pulled tightly over the window and realized she was in the bed at Paradise. She heard her mother's voice.

"Adam!" Louise whispered loudly. "She's coming around, I think."

"Mother," Emmaline said, and her voice grated, her throat dry and her tongue thick and parched. "What are you doing here?"

Louise smiled through the tears in her eyes and ran a hand over Emmaline's face. "Adam is here, darling. Adam is here."

She turned her head to him as he moved his chair close to the bed and picked up her hand. She heard the door to the bedroom close and knew they were alone. Just the two of them. Adam looked as if he'd been up for days on end. His beard was thick and his hair wild and standing on end. There were dark circles under his eyes and he looked at her with such worry and concern, she was frightened.

"What is it, Adam? What has happened?"

He licked his lips and stared at her for the longest time. "We lost the baby, Emmaline. A baby boy. Dr. Carter said he was not fully formed as he should have been."

"The baby? Our baby?"

Adam nodded. "Dr. Carter will be back within the hour. I'm sure your mother sent for him. He'll want to examine you."

"But why? Our baby is dead?" She felt hopelessness bear down on her and the beginnings of misery and pain that she could see on her horizon.

"You've lost a lot of blood. We . . . we weren't sure if you would ever wake up"—he examined her hand—"it's been two days and a half since you delivered him."

"I want to see him, Adam," she said with some urgency. "I want to see." She tried pitifully to pull the blankets away from herself. But she was exhausted just from the knowledge. She could no more climb out of the bed than flap her arms and fly up to the sky.

"He's buried, Emmaline. In the Paradise cemetery. Jim and Matt made a little . . . box for him"—he looked up at her with watery eyes—"He was no bigger than my palm."

Then she heard someone crying and moaning and realized it was her. She slept fitfully then after the doctor left, no doubt aided by whatever her mother had given her at his direction.

* * *

EMMALINE PULLED HERSELF UP TO A SITTING POSITION AGAINST the wooden headboard of the bed. She'd woken sometime before and stayed in bed remembering everything that had happened in the last two weeks as she'd done every morning. The baby was gone. The baby was gone and buried. She felt empty, as if all the hope and wonder and terror she'd felt was gone. Was it logical to miss terror? Yes. She thought it might be, as any feeling would be preferable to nothingness.

But there was something else there she'd just begun to identify. She wasn't relieved the baby was gone. That was not it at all as she'd begun to think about milestones with the child, and with Adam. She'd begun to think about when this little boy or girl would reach up and touch her face or smile or discover his or her toes. She'd begun to think about more children, a family sitting down to a meal with Adam at his usual place and her in Mrs. Gentry's seat. She'd been desperately trying to imagine herself and her husband in the future being happy and satisfied with what they'd both settled for.

But there was relief if she was honest with herself. She'd not have to endure sly looks and comments for her or the child, maybe for all of her life. She'd not have to pretend that this marriage was anything but a salvation of reputation for her and respite from the bruising grip of grief that consumed Adam.

She pulled her legs out from under the blankets and turned to sit on the side of the bed. Sometimes it felt as if her innards were going to fall out from between her legs if she were to take too jaunty a step, and her breasts were still a bit sore. Otherwise she was fine, and it was very sad to feel fine, she thought. She'd convinced herself since she'd lost their son that she should be in terrible pain. Thinking however empty she felt in those moments, at some point she would be swamped with grief and anger and guilt and shouldn't her physical self be in tune with her emotional self? Wouldn't it be easier to drift away from everyone if her bones and her soul both ached in rhythm?

But today was a new day, she was feeling more herself, and she was not going to wallow. She was going to pick herself up and reexamine everything. If she'd learned anything, it was that she needed to make some changes. Raising a family had never been her goal, not that she wouldn't have liked children, but it wasn't the total of her life as it seemed to be with Nettie. She needed to find out what she wanted her future to look like. She looked around the bedroom and realized she couldn't do that here, in this room, with Adam close by and the shadow of their marriage over her like a cloud. Her marriage. If there was any speck of something positive, it would be that they would both be released from this awkward, forced union.

She had some money in the bank, everything that she'd received from her father's will, as all her brothers and sisters had, the yearly dividends they all received from Somerset Farriers, and everything she'd earned helping Marabelle at the mercantile. It wasn't a fortune, but it was not a small amount, either. She could move away and begin again, perhaps to Washington, like Mrs. Gentry had, or New York even with Aunt Madge, or maybe Philadelphia where she could truly reach for her dream. She stood up, happy that she wasn't dizzy. She went to the bathing room and filled the tub.

* * *

"WHAT?" ADAM SAID TO JENNY A WEEK LATER EVEN AS HE watched George wrestle a new foal that had been born with the cord wrapped twice around its neck. "Careful George. The mare's trying to get up."

"Mrs. Gentry is packed and leaving."

Adam turned from where he stood in the entrance to a stall. "My mother went to Washington weeks ago now. Are you saying she's come home?"

Jenny shook her head impatiently. "Your wife. Your wife told Beatrice not to bother calling for the carriage, that she could walk to Winchester."

"Emmaline? Emmaline is going to walk to Winchester."

"Yes. That's what she said."

Adam watched as Jenny walked away from him. "I've got to check on my wife, George. Are we in good shape until the next one drops?"

"We're good, Mr. Gentry. I don't think we're going to have another birth until tomorrow or longer."

"Get me, George, whenever it happens."

Adam slapped the straw off his pant legs with his hat as he walked to the house. He was glad Emmaline was up and moving around even though the doctor had told her to stay in bed for one more week. She was asleep every night when he went to bed and he was gone to the stables before she was awake in the morning, so they'd not talked at all other than some pleasantries when he'd turned up to share his coffee with her after dinner as he'd been eating with George in the bunkhouse the entire week. She'd been getting her strength back and eating well according to Mabel.

He walked in the back door, scraped his boots on the rug, and went through the kitchen to the front hallway. Emmaline stood there in a brown skirt, white shirtwaist, and a loose black jacket with a carpet bag sitting at her feet. What was she doing?

"Emmaline?" He walked down the hall toward her. Beatrice glanced at him and hurried away. The house was silent all around him as if its occupants had sensed a storm about to break. "Jenny said you needed to go to Winchester. Are you up to it?"

"Oh, hello, Adam," she said, as she fiddled nervously with hooks on her jacket. "I'm feeling well. Thank you. I've left you a note in your room."

"A note?"

"I could never thank you enough for rescuing me and thereby rescuing my family. You were truly a hero, just as I always thought," she said hurriedly and breathlessly as if she'd been rehearsing it. She looked away quickly and picked up her bag.

He didn't move out of her way. "What is in the note, Emmaline?"

"A thank-you of course"—her eyes slid away from his—"and my permission, my blessing really, not that you need it, to get an annulment or a divorce or whatever is expedient."

Adam shook his head. "What are you talking about?"

"There is no need for you to sacrifice yourself anymore. The baby . . . our baby is gone."

"So, that's it? We lost a child and that's it?" Adam said, his voice rising.

"There's no need to torture ourselves. We've never consummated the marriage so there'll never be any awkwardness between us. I plan on leaving Winchester in a week or two."

He was inching close to her, so angry, so . . . disappointed, so hurt, that he was having trouble holding his temper and remaining civil. He never lost his temper, he thought briefly, but then he looked at her hand.

"Where are your engagement and wedding rings?"

"I left them with the note. It didn't seem right . . ."

"It isn't right." His voice rose with each word. "You're my wife and you should wear the damn rings."

Her face flushed. "There's no need to shout. I'm trying to make this easy for both of us."

He stalked closer to her. "There is every reason to shout. My wife is sneaking off behind my back and leaving me. I think that's plenty of goddamned reason to shout."

Emmaline's mouth dropped open and her eyes widened. "I'm not afraid of you, Adam Gentry! There's no reason for us to remain together now after my miscarriage. I'm going to start anew somewhere else, and you'll be able to put all of this behind you. You'll have time to heal over the loss of Josephine and your child."

"I don't expect you to be afraid of me and I'll holler all I want in my own home!" Adam bellowed and threw his hat on the floor. He stepped within inches of her. "You're my wife. That's it. We're married for better or worse."

"Why are you being so unreasonable?" She backed up as he stalked forward, until she was flush against the wall. "You can't think you wish to be married to me!"

"You don't know what the hell I'm thinking," Adam growled as he leaned close to her face. Her cheeks were red, and her eyes flashing and determined. "Maybe we should consummate this marriage right now!"

She took in a sharp breath and brought her hand up from her side, aiming to slap his face. He caught it and pushed it against the wall over her shoulder. He leaned close to her, close enough to see the gold flecks in her brown eyes and feel the heat of her against him. It was as if he was watching himself from afar as this couldn't be his normal, orderly persona. He was furious with her and fully aroused in his coarse work pants. She looked at his mouth, and he lost all semblance of control.

Adam kissed her roughly, her hand held above her head, slipping his tongue in her mouth, hearing himself moan as he did, tilting her head back until it touched the wall and grabbing her waist, pulling her hips forward against him. He opened his eyes long enough to see her lashes drift up and down, wafting like a mating call, sensuous and primitive.

She brought her other hand slowly up his chest and lingered there, running her fingers across his flannel shirt, and kissing him back, growling as she did. She lifted her foot from the floor and moved her leg up his shin, past his knee until the inside of her thigh was resting against the outside of his. He moved between her legs with his hip, rubbing her, and had just palmed her breast, running a thumb over a taut nipple when he heard someone behind them.

"Adam?" he heard his sister-in-law say. He felt Emmaline's leg slide down his as he released her hand from the wall.

He turned, keeping Emmaline out of Annie's and Matt's views. Annie covered her open mouth with her hand, and Matt didn't even try to contain his laughter. Adam swallowed.

"Annie's been worried about you two!" Matt looked at his wife. "I told you there was nothing to worry about."

"We'll be going," Annie said quickly. "I just wanted to check on you. The last time I was here Emmaline seemed . . . to be feeling sad."

"I'm thinking she's not sad anymore." Matt grinned, but Annie was already pulling him out the door.

Adam could hear his brother's laughter still. He turned to Emmaline, feeling wildly out of control and nervous. "I don't know what came over me," he said. "I was rude and forward and I richly deserved the slap you were planning on. I'm sorry. Can we continue this discussion in the main room?"

She was staring at him as if he'd never met her, as if he were a complete stranger to her. He understood her confusion. He was barely able to recognize himself.

"Stay here, please," he said and waited for her nod. He swiped his hat from the floor and went out through the kitchens until he saw Jenny and Mabel and Beatrice in the kitchen garden, all looking at him skeptically.

"I'd like a coffee tray and some biscuits in the main room, please," he said.

Mabel hurried toward him. "I have a pot on and will bring it right away, Mr. Adam."

Adam found Emmaline in the same spot in the entranceway where he'd left her. Her cheeks were no longer pink, but her hair was mussed, and her lips looked as if she'd been thoroughly kissed and a bit more. "Will you join me in the main room?"

She followed him, and he waited for her to seat herself as Mabel bustled in with a tray. Adam poured a cup of coffee, added one sugar and a healthy splash of cream, and handed it to her. She sat it on the side table and looked at him. He heard the door close as Mabel left.

"Why are you leaving?" he blurted out before he could think better of it.

"The baby is gone, Adam. I will never forget your kindness to me, but it's no longer necessary."

Adam seated himself. "I took vows at the church a few weeks ago and you were standing right beside me. We're married."

"But the entire reason we're married no longer exists."

Adam most often was the one who listened as someone bared their soul. He was able to dissect what others said about how they felt and why. He was able to give good advice and yet be honest and always encouraging. It was gift, he felt. His mother had it and he'd watched her wield her influence since he was a young boy. But he was adrift right now. He couldn't handle the overwhelming sense of isolation and disillusionment he felt when he realized Emmaline was leaving him. Leaving their marriage. Words tumbled out of his mouth then, much to his mortification.

"Josephine is gone and our child with her. I can barely write to her brother, a dear friend for years, as I cannot scribble niceties to him without any mention of his sister. Mother has moved to Washington. Matt and Livie are married and in their own homes. Jenny and Mabel are seriously considering retiring from their work here at Paradise." He looked up at her then. "Our child is gone, cold in a grave. And now, you want to leave me, too."

She stared at him, blinking and licking her lips. He stood and went to the window to study the landscape rather than consider the foolish and ridiculous words he'd just spoken but couldn't have stopped himself from saying.

There was an open lonely chasm in his chest. How silly it was to be so sensitive, as if he weren't a man with significant responsibilities and prospects, but there was no closing that empty space it seemed. He'd wondered if he was meant to be alone in this world after Josephine's death. But his marriage to Emmaline, ragtag as it was, had dangled some thin thread of possibility that he could have a partner, and even though he'd convinced himself he was saving her perhaps she was saving him instead. He turned when she cleared her throat and found her standing beside him gazing out at the landscape, too.

"I don't know what I'm about, Adam. I've got to find out what it is, and I have a suspicion it's not having children, not right now anyway."

"What do you mean?"

She shrugged. "I've never been like Nettie or Betsy, dreaming of starting a family in their own home. Painting walls and mending clothes. Wiping runny noses and teaching a primer. I was prepared to do all that with this child, although it wouldn't be the same as living in the small house Edwin has leased for him and Betsy. But she is thrilled beyond belief, Mother says, to do all those things. To be a wife and a mother at the exclusion of everything else. Nettie is the same."

"What is it you want then?"

She looked up at him, and he was reminded of the kiss they'd shared just minutes ago. He'd been intolerably forward but she'd taken to that heated embrace, he was experienced enough to know.

"I'm not sure, Adam. There are things about me that no one knows." She looked away. "Things that I may want to pursue."

"What are these things? Perhaps I can help."

"I doubt that. I'll never be able to continue them if I'm to be a wife and mother and mistress of this massive home. Not to say it's not magnificent because it is. Paradise is quite exceptional as I'm sure you know but the running of it, the maintenance of it, surely took the majority of your mother's day, let alone raising three children. I can't do what I want and do this, too." She looked up at him. "That's why I'm releasing you. You need someone as competent and committed as Mrs. Gentry."

"You believe then that my father and mother were happy together because she kept this house, expanded it several times, raised us, directed staff, and all the other things she did that I have no idea of?"

"Mrs. Gentry made a comfortable place for her husband to come home to and saw to her children's education. Of course, it led to their happiness. My mother has emphasized repeatedly to my sisters and I to do exactly that to ensure marital bliss, as she refers to it."

"Marital bliss?" He couldn't help the smile curving his lips.

"Nettie says marital bliss occurs in the bedroom and rarely in any other room of the house."

"Your sister is quite outspoken, isn't she?"

"You have no idea."

"Do you think you'll ever want those things, Emmaline? The runny noses and the primers?"

"I do. But not right at this moment. Please don't think poorly of me."

"I don't think poorly of you, and I admit that I anticipated few changes in my life after marriage. That you would manage the household and any children. That I would continue on doing exactly as I have always done. But that may not be the way of our marriage."

There was a knock at the door and Jenny came in the room. "I beg your pardon for interrupting you, Mr. Adam. I was wondering if it will just be the two of you for dinner."

He looked down at Emmaline and spoke softly. "Will you stay for dinner? Please?"

CHAPTER 7

Emmaline couldn't gather her thoughts. Bits of her brain were crashing into one another, with no regard for her sense and intelligence. How in the world did Adam end up kissing her? They'd been screaming at each other and wrapped around each other in the next moment. And now they were talking to each other in an intimate way about things she preferred left unsaid—exactly in the way she'd imagined her perfect husband would speak to her. She'd already told him he could divorce her and that she didn't really wish to raise his children. She might as well continue to embrace honesty. It was a promise she'd made to herself that very morning.

"Jenny?" she said and cleared her throat.

"Yes, Miss Emmaline? I can have the dining room ready by five."

"Would it be too much trouble to bring us a tray of whatever you are preparing in here? I'll have some of that cold tea you served this morning, rather than this coffee, as well, please." She looked at Adam. "Would you like anything special to drink?"

He stared at her for the longest time. "I'll have whatever Mrs. Gentry is having."

"Right away," Jenny said even as she wrung her hands together.

Emmaline blew a breath. "I imagine I've set the kitchen on its ear, but I am hungry, and I don't really feel like sitting so far away from each other at that massive table if we are to have a conversation." She pulled off her jacket, stepped out of her shoes, and sat down on one of the soft chairs in front of the fireplace. She stood back up and removed what was sitting on a small table near a chair by the window. She dragged the table between the two chairs and sat again, pulling her feet under her. Adam was still standing.

"Perhaps you aren't hungry. I'm ravenous."

"I've not changed for dinner."

She shrugged. "It's your house, Adam. Take your boots off and sit down. What we're discussing calls for comfort, I think, rather than formality."

He slowly rounded the chair and stood in front of her. "It's your house, too."

"Hardly. I appreciate your intentions to include me, but I've not left your rooms for more than a few hours since our wedding. But that's hardly what we need to discuss."

She watched him sit down as if the chair would break in half if he put his full weight to it and found her eyes straying to that part of him he'd been rubbing between her legs. How strange to think of him in this way! When she'd thought about having marital relations with him, she'd imagined the lifting of her thickest flannel nightgown in a darkened room and a few obligatory kisses on the cheek followed by an awkward squeeze of her breast. Some gentlemanly and kind words of thanks and praise. How embarrassing it would have been to face each other the following morning over coffee! But she could feel the heat of a flush on her neck and face when she recalled how he'd looked at her as his mouth had claimed hers. It had been as if they were both on fire!

Jenny came into the main room leading Beatrice carrying a

large tray. "Here, Beatrice. Sit it here between us. Oh, how delicious this looks!"

Emmaline picked up a roll and tossed it from one hand to the other. "These are hot!" she said and smiled up at Jenny as the two women left the room. "And they smell delicious!"

Emmaline pulled the steaming, yeasty-smelling roll apart and stuffed a piece of turkey breast between the halves. She placed one of the linen napkins on her lap and sat back in her seat, watching the low flames in the fireplace ahead of her. She could become accustomed to the service here at Paradise. Her parents' household employed a cook and a housekeeper but with her mother, two sisters, and a brother still at home, she was accustomed to doing many of the everyday chores. Having a meal delivered to her side, especially one as tempting as this one as she'd just spied small plates with slabs of butter cake with chocolate frosting on the tray, was a real treat. She licked her fingers and glanced at Adam. He was staring at her.

"We're not getting divorced," he said finally.

"I'm not the right wife for you."

"How could you possibly know if you are right for me? We've barely gotten to know each other. It's a moot point anyway. We're married. There'll be no other wives for me."

Emmaline looked at him. She couldn't say that he didn't bring out certain emotions within her, many of which she was unaccustomed to feeling, empathy being the most notable. She felt sorry him. His tragic speech about everyone leaving him was the only reason she was still here, at Paradise, that was, eating roast turkey and deviled eggs and drinking cold tea. She wasn't certain she'd ever heard a person express such a sad opinion of themselves, especially as it had come from Adam Gentry, who was the very definition of self-possessed and poised. So, she had stayed.

"Will you stop me from leaving then?" She was suddenly aware that she was no longer under the auspices of a mother who was easily manipulated or an older brother who was blind to everything going on around him other than his wife, especially now that Olivia was expecting.

He stared at her for the longest time, making her palms sweat and her heart beat in double time, thinking of giving up everything she'd worked so hard for. She'd been prepared to have this child and others and raise them and run a household, if for no other reason than that she owed him. But she'd been terrified she'd end up unhappy and shrill in her complaints, as the weight of what she'd sacrificed would bear down on her.

"No. I'll not stop you from leaving," he whispered and sat back in his chair, staring straight ahead, but seeing little, if she were to guess.

She breathed a sigh of relief. "Thank you." Then she looked over at him. Tendrils of guilt were winding their way around her middle. He looked so forlorn, so unlike the confident Adam she knew. It was heady to think that she had any effect on him let alone this look he wore, but it nearly broke her heart. This was the man who was willing to be a father to a child he'd not conceived and had cried when that child had died. The same man who had married her to protect her and save her honor.

"You looked so ragged when I woke up after I lost the baby, Adam," she said softly. "You're looking the same now. We couldn't mean that much to you."

He glanced at her and was silent for a long few minutes. "I didn't think you were going to wake up. We've never acted as if this was a love affair like Livie and Jim, but it was still my marriage. You are still my wife. Those vows mean something, and I thought I'd lost that when you lay there white-faced and still. You're my future, Emmaline, and my commitment to you was made the day I put that ring on your finger. The loss of our child was terrible enough without the thought of losing my wife."

She stared at him, listening to his declaration and feeling small and petty. She'd made the same commitment and was not honoring her end of the bargain, it seemed. Could she compromise? Could he?

"I've been selfish," she said. "I've been chasing a dream around for ages that burned away the moment I realized I was expecting. You rescued me and now that there's a chance that I can pursue that dream again, I've been focused solely on myself with small regard to our marriage. Truthfully, it meant little to me other than a way to save face, to be comfortable, to have a father for the child, and to save my family the shame."

"Your brother said you were brutally honest. He wasn't joking, was he?"

She shook her head slowly. "He was not."

"I'll write you a check, Emmaline. Chase this dream of yours. I'll not stop you."

She watched him walk out of the room and pull the door closed behind him. She'd never felt so foolish, so angry, so confused in her life, even including being an unwed woman expecting a child. What had she done? Had she turned away from a man so honorable that he would rescue her and release her all the same? And she could not, she could absolutely not, get the vision of him coming close to her to kiss her out of her head. That kiss had affected her in ways she'd not considered before. Suddenly, Adam Gentry was a man, not merely a person older than she who was never in her thoughts when she considered something as intimate as touching mouths. But after that kiss, she could picture him in no other way than as a virile and attractive man.

She licked her lips thinking about the way it felt to have Adam kiss her. It was nothing like the sloppy and slipshod meeting of lips with that dunderhead Henry, who'd gotten her with child. Although exciting at the time, rash as it had been, she'd wondered then if his clinking of teeth followed by a tongue as large as a dill pickle invading her mouth was the very best the kissing world had to offer. She knew now with certainty that it was not.

. . .

EMMALINE HADN'T LEFT. ADAM WAS SURPRISED WHEN HE CAME back from the stables late in the evening and found her at the small desk in the main room, her carpet bag sitting near the settee. He stood looking at her for quite some time. Her hair was coming down on one side of her head and one sleeve of her shirt was rolled up and one rolled down and still buttoned at the cuff. One shoe was lying on its side, presumably toed off as she walked to the desk, the other, out of sight. Was that a stocking draped over the back of her chair? His mother and sister were always neat and put together, even when doing heavy or hot chores. Emmaline looked as if a strong wind had blown by, rearranging her clothing and hair and she hadn't the slightest inclination to set herself to rights. She was talking softly to herself. He wondered what she was concentrating on so intently, her pen scratching away on a paper in front of her, other sheets scattered around her feet on the floor.

She was nothing like the always perfectly groomed Josephine, but he couldn't deny that she was incredibly appealing to him in her disorder, and what a strange thought to have about his young wife. The one he'd kissed as if she were a saloon girl as she'd run her leg up his side.

"I thought you'd be gone by now."

She turned around in her seat and looked at him and then past him, out the window. "Oh. What time is it? It's almost dark out. I think Jenny came in and lit the lamps."

"She would have."

She hurriedly stacked her sheets of paper into a pile, bending over to gather up the ones on the floor and throw them into the fireplace. He wanted to ask her what she was doing. He wanted to ask her why she hadn't left. He wanted to tell her he was glad she was still here.

"I'm going to the kitchen to see if there is anything in the icebox to eat after I wash up. Are you hungry?"

She stood then and looked at him. "Is that blood on your shirt?"

He nodded. "I've been helping George with the foals."

"Ah."

"Would you like me to call for the carriage? I will, if you'd prefer to go back to your mother's this evening."

She shook her head. "No. Not unless you want me to."

"I don't. I'm glad you've stayed. For however long," he said and thought he was telling the truth.

"I could eat more of those rolls and that turkey, and I never did have a slice of cake." She tilted her head and smiled.

Her grin gut-punched him. There were just no formalities where she was concerned. No flirting words or coquettish reluctance when it came to food or her state of dress or anything really. She was just Emmaline. This was what Jim had been talking about. She would have a difficult time with a husband who was rigid in his rules for marriage and wifely duties and attitudes. And what were *his* expectations now that that thought occurred to him? What did he want from her? From this union? He didn't think any of his prior notions would stand up to this marriage. If it was to work, and the more he thought about that kiss, the more he was convinced that their marriage deserved a chance, he needed to open his mind to new possibilities.

He found her in the kitchen drinking a glass of tea, her head titled back, her eyes closed as if she was parched.

"That is so delicious, and I was so thirsty. Would you like some?" she asked as she filled her glass from the pitcher on the table and handed it to him.

"I can get my own glass, Emmaline. This is yours."

She shrugged. "There'll be less dishes for us to wash if we share."

He took the glass and drank from it, feeling as if there was some odd intimacy at play. He watched her unwrap a turkey leg and put it on a plate beside the butter and a few rolls. She sat down without looking at him and cut the leg in several places making it easy to pull the meat off with her fingers. She looked up at him.

"I thought you were hungry."

He pulled out a chair and sat. She was not unmannerly. She was taking small bites and chewing and wiping her fingers on the towel she'd placed between them. She was just not as formal as he was accustomed to. She knew how to act at a dining room table. He'd seen her do just that with refined manners.

"I'm trying to remember the last time I sat at this table," he said. "It's been years."

"We all sat around the kitchen table in the mornings at my house. Mother didn't of course, she took her warmed chocolate in her rooms. Father would lean against the stove and drink his coffee and we would chatter about school or what we'd be doing that day. Helen would dip out the porridge or grill bread with honey and we would drink cold milk."

"We ate our meals in a small dining room that was part of this kitchen until Mother had the formal dining room built. But this little two-seat table has been here forever, I think since Mother and Father moved here. They had coffee together at this table in the afternoons most days. Matt and I would sit here when Mabel was baking, and Livie, too, when she was old enough, hoping for a treat."

"Did Mabel ever disappoint?"

"Never."

She smiled. "All and all, I had a lovely childhood. I think you did, too."

"I did. Father was strict about some things, our work with the horses or helping Mother, but he was just as likely to be dancing a jig in the middle of the barns. He was a happy and passionate man. Quick to do his share and just as quick to tell a silly story. Matt reminds me of him."

"I remember watching him at our house one holiday party, I was ten or so, I suppose." She looked at Adam. "He was so obviously and completely enamored with your mother. Nettie and I watched them from where we sat on the staircase and Nettie, she was maybe thirteen and just becoming interested in boys, said that her husband was going to look at her like your father looked at your mother. He'd stared at her and smiled, touching her back or holding her hand, and looking around the room as if to say he was the luckiest man on earth."

"Nettie married the right man, then," Adam said with a chuckle. "John has been watching her since he was thirteen, just about the time he started noticing girls."

"They are perfect together. What other man could live with Nettie and not kill her?"

Adam laughed out loud. "I've always liked Nettie and Jim. I don't know your younger sisters and brothers very well at all. Maybe I'll get to know them a bit better now."

Emmaline wiped her fingers and dabbed her mouth with the napkin she had draped over her lap. She looked up at him.

"Or maybe not," he said ruefully. "Would you like me to call for the gig?"

She shook her head and stood. He watched as she wrapped the turkey leg and put it in the icebox. She picked up the plates they'd used and took them to the sink, running water over them and the glass they'd shared and soaping up the scrap of linen that lay draped over the edge of the sink. She turned slightly and tossed him the red-striped linen kitchen towel from the hook on the side of the oak cabinet. Apparently, he was to dry the dishes and the fork and the glass. He did and sat them on the ridged side of the porcelain sink that had been recently installed.

Adam followed her, extinguishing the kerosene lamps as he went, up the steps, down the long quiet hallway, as she carried her shoes she'd picked up from the main room in one hand and her stockings in the other. She was staying at least one more night, and he was glad of it.

CHAPTER 8

Emmaline walked directly into the bathing room, washed her face and hands, used her tooth powder, and changed into her favorite nightgown. She'd been wearing voluminous long-sleeved flannel ones when in bed before as it seemed she was always cold, but she wasn't anymore. One more sign that she was back to her old self, she thought as she pulled the lightweight linen nightgown over her head. It was short-sleeved and scoop-necked and fell to just below her knees where she'd cut it off and paid Betsy to hem it. She untangled her hair with her fingers and loosely braided it.

She thought about how ridiculous her plan that morning had been, to leave a note to explain to her husband why she'd left him. She was a coward, she thought. She'd not wanted to have direct conversations, but they'd had them anyway and although nothing was resolved, she'd not crept out of the house like she was guilty of some crime. She was glad they'd talked and glad she hadn't left. How strange, considering she was convinced she didn't want to discuss anything with him and hadn't been able pack her bag fast enough to make her getaway.

Adam was changed into his drawstring drawers and long john shirt and turned from where he was pulling down the blankets on their bed when she came out of the bathing room. He looked at her slowly from her head to her toes. Maybe he missed the eleven yards of yellow checked flannel that she'd worn since their wedding. She sat at the vanity and rubbed thick cream onto her hands hoping to get the ink from her leaking fountain pen to rub off of her fingertips.

They climbed into bed at the same time, back to back, not touching of course, and she closed her eyes thinking about Adam's broad chest and the way his cotton shirt stretched across it.

EMMALINE WAS HAVING A DELICIOUS DREAM. HER BREASTS were rubbing against a solid wall of male chest and her hips were surging against heat in a slow rhythm. Her nightgown was around her waist and a muscled leg was edging itself between her knees. She could feel soft flannel on her inner thigh as the leg inched its way up until it was cradled against her. It was remarkably satisfying to rub herself on those thick muscles and no matter how hard or fast she moved, it stayed pressed against her, giving no quarter. Her breasts were aching, feeling swollen, itching for something she could not identify in her semiconscious state.

Then a hand came around her breast, squeezing and rubbing, finally closing over her nipple, tugging with a thumb and forefinger. She moaned deep and low in her throat, feeling the sound in the pit of her stomach, moving her hips faster and faster. Her eyes fluttered open, her face against wiry, dark hair that tickled, where it stuck out of the neck of a shirt. The feeling only increased her need and the speed of her hips, but she was awake then, clutching the soft cotton stretched tight over a broad back. She reached down to the firm bum attached to that thigh and held it, taking short breaths and reaching for something she didn't know how to find.

The hand on her breast moved down her stomach, between

her legs, replacing the muscled thigh. Fingers played over her and she realized she was wet there, she could hear it and feel it. A long finger went inside her, and a thumb moved nearby in a slow circle making her cry out as the conscious world went blank and she fell, head over heels, in pleasure.

She was fully awake when the warmth left her. It was Adam, of course, breathing in pants, lying on his back now, his hands clutching the sheets. She looked down his body in the dim, gray morning light to where that part of him, his penis, she thought and held in a giggle, strained against his drawstring pants.

"Can I touch it?" she whispered.

He groaned but didn't open his eyes or unclench his fists, his forearms hard and showing veins from his efforts. She reached over to him and untied the cord around his waist, moving his drawers down as lifted his bum from the mattress. He sprang free and she couldn't stop herself from staring at that part of him, standing straight out of dark curly hair, long and thick and puls-ing. She touched him before she could think what she was doing, and he moaned, his arm thrown over his eyes. She wrapped her hand around the length of the soft skin and ran a thumb up to its crown. Her legs shifted, and she felt empty and aching for his touch again. His hips began to pump against her hand and she recognized its eroticism for what it was and couldn't stop herself from thinking she wanted to kiss him there, on the tip of him. He jerked his shirt above his stomach and clenched his fist around hers, moving her hand faster, tight around him. His shoulders came off the bed and he released with a guttural moan.

She'd had no idea, she thought as she watched him roll up to a sitting position and head to the water closet without one look at her. No damnable idea of the power and the intimacy that she would feel.

That idiot Henry with his pickle tongue and his fumblings. One minute he was kissing her ear, licking it rather, and the next he had himself in hand and her skirts up. There had been *one* hard push, dry flesh forcing its way past her entrance, her curse, and the pain that followed. He'd stood up then, fastening his buttons; she was amazed when she looked back that babies were made in mere seconds.

She'd had some idea that the act was a bit more, that she'd feel something for the other person, but her experience said no. But this . . . this hot intimacy was so much more than her wildest fantasies and strangely, she couldn't imagine doing it with anyone other than Adam, which was just as well since she was married to him. He padded back into the bedroom, climbed in bed, and rolled up on his side to face her, looking grim.

ADAM SEARCHED HER FACE FOR DISMAY OR EMBARRASSMENT. HE saw none of those things, although he didn't know her moods and wasn't able to anticipate her reactions all that well. He was on shaky ground himself, having experienced what many would say was a strange, if incomplete, consummation of a marriage.

"I'm sorry, Emmaline," he said finally. "I didn't mean to spoil your plans."

"What do you mean 'spoil my plans'?"

"Well, now that the marriage has been consummated—"

"But we really didn't do that, did we?" she interrupted.

He took a deep breath and thought plain speech was required even as he resisted saying what was necessary. "I touched you," he said and swallowed. "I touched you intimately. There is no going back. We don't do what we did and act as if it is nothing."

"I touched you, too." She tucked a hand under her pillow.

He nodded. "Yes. Yes, you did, and that is why you can't walk away from this marriage. Yesterday I told you I'd give you money to go chase your dream, even if that wasn't what I wanted to happen, but now, things are different."

"I'll have to think on that," she said and proceeded to roll over, giving him her back.

"There's nothing to think about, Emmaline." His eyes trailed down her body to her waist, the perfect flare of her hips, and her long legs that had been wrapped around his. He nearly groaned just thinking of it.

She looked over her shoulder at him. "Your penis never went inside me. We never did what was necessary to have babies, although I enjoyed this very much. You needn't feel obligated."

He closed his eyes. "I am absolutely obligated. I'm your husband. I've touched you and you've . . ."

"Touched your penis. It's very soft, the skin I mean. What a peculiar thing." She glanced down. "It just comes and goes."

Adam barked a laugh. He couldn't help himself. "It doesn't just come and go." She was smiling at him and he was certain this was the oddest conversation he'd ever had. "I mean, it does, but it happens because I'm aroused."

She looked at him then from under her lashes, as if she was a siren of old, as if she had the sexual experience of the most expensive lady of the evening in New York City. He licked his lips.

"I had the strangest desire to kiss it."

He did groan then and could feel himself get hard.

"And there it is again." She stared at that part of him.

"You've got to stop looking at it and talking about it," he said sternly even though he was feeling amused and a bit ridiculous. "And where did you hear that word?"

"Penis? What should I call it?"

Adam took a deep breath and spoke slowly. "Where did you hear that word, Emmaline?"

"I found some books in a trunk in Jim's room when I was cleaning one day."

"Books? What type of books?"

"One was from the Far East with a strange name, but I didn't have time to examine it. The other was a medical journal"—she looked up at him—"with pictures."

"With pictures?"

She nodded. "I didn't get to look at either of them as much as I would have liked because the trunk was locked every other time I moved the bed to change the sheets. And then it was gone."

"Did you show anyone else the books?"

"Good Lord, no! Nettie would have wanted to discuss it at dinner and Betsy would have fainted away from blushing."

"And that's where you saw the word."

"It was very clearly marked, and the drawing"—she glanced at his crotch—"was remarkably accurate."

Of all the strange things that had happened over the course of that day, Adam feeling the heat of a blush on his cheeks was the strangest. He was laughing, too, blushing and laughing as if he were a fifteen-year-old girl with her first beau.

"I can't stop thinking about Nettie at your dinner table discussing . . ."

"Penises," she said and laughed along with him.

Their laughter faded, and Adam sat up on the side of the bed, his back to his wife. "Later today I want to talk about your dreams. About what you'd prefer to do other than be married to me."

ADAM SPENT THE DAY IN THE BARNS HELPING GEORGE AND WAS thankful that the things he was doing didn't not require much active thought. They were tasks he'd done hundreds of times, although he'd often been the one directing the activities. George took one look at him that morning and began to give orders to the other stable men about what needed to be done with the new foals and the still-expectant mares.

"Hand me that clamp there, if you would," George said and waited. "Mr. Gentry?"

Adam was having difficulty not thinking about Emmaline. She was far different than he'd expected and far more interesting, too. Life would never be boring, that was for certain, and he was genuinely curious to know what she'd been writing when he found her at the desk in the main room. He was certain it had something to do with these dreams of hers.

"Mr. Gentry?"

Adam grabbed the clamp and handed it to George. "Sorry."

George smiled and then turned to continue with his work. "Mrs. Gentry feeling better, sir?"

Good God! Adam thought. He was mostly likely the subject of some unseemly speculation as he was unable to concentrate for longer than a minute and had actually walked into a partially opened barn door as he thought about their early morning awakening and didn't watch where he was stepping. She was all pent-up passion with no maidenly modesty, but she was artless as well. There was nothing planned or contrived about Emmaline's sexuality.

"Much better," he said. "In fact, if all is in hand here, I'm going to see if Mrs. Gentry is setting out a luncheon."

George nodded and smiled again, with a wink. "Yes, sir."

Adam walked out of the barn with as much dignity as he could muster, careful to step through the door rather than into it. He found Emmaline back at the writing desk in the main room. She was laughing softly as he approached.

"Something must be silly enough to make you laugh like that," he said as he came to stand beside the desk among discarded pieces of paper.

She looked up at him and smiled. "There *was* something silly enough, and I wrote it. There is no greater feeling than when the words I put on paper have meaning and provoke a response, whether it's laughter or tears or terror. Even though I'm the one writing them."

It was apparent that there was much more to his young bride

than he'd thought a month ago, or even a week ago. It didn't seem as if she was prepared to share more of what she was doing as they stared at each other and he sensed she would have to make her own decision as to when to take him into her confidences. "Have you had your lunch?"

"No. I haven't." She turned around in her seat. "I'd like to go into town before we eat. Would you care to join me?"

"I would. Let me change. Are you missing your mother and sisters? It has been a while since we've visited with them."

"Dear Lord, no. Although we can stop if you insist."

"I don't insist. Where will we be going? Do I need to change into something more presentable?"

She shook her head and bent to gather papers, after capping her fountain pen. "You don't need to change unless you are concerned with what Mrs. Witherspoon thinks of you."

"You have something to be telegraphed or mailed?"

"Something has been delivered for me, actually."

"Let me get the gig."

A few minutes later, they were seated side by side and on their way to Winchester. He glanced over at her and found her looking off into the forest of trees, and then looking closely at Matt and Annie's home as they rode by as if she was hoping to see one of them.

"It's a beautiful day," he said and thought that comment was about as trite a thing as he could utter, but he was feeling out of his depths and didn't know what else to say. Which was ridiculous as he was an adult man with a decade more living under his belt than her. And it gnawed at him. He sensed he couldn't charm Emmaline. He couldn't coax her or compliment her or guide her in the direction he wanted her to go. She would go the direction she chose, with him or without him.

"It is," she said and lifted her face up to the sun. "It feels like summer is finally here for good."

He turned his head to look at her. Her dark hair was shining and waving and pulled back loosely with a ribbon. She had a long neck, a strong chin, and a perfect nose with just a dusting of freckles. Her eyes were dark brown with streaks of lighter color, as if someone had stirred molasses, fringed with long lashes, meant to make him want to kiss her until neither of them could breathe. She was beautiful, even dressed in her drab gray, high-necked dress. She was his wife. And he hadn't the foggiest notion of how to proceed with his marriage or if there was to be any marriage at all.

EMMALINE WAS SICK TO HER STOMACH. NOT LIKE SHE'D BEEN when she'd been expecting a child, thank goodness, but nevertheless, feeling as if the bread and jelly she'd eaten that morning were going to reappear in her lap. She was sweating and doing everything in her power to not flap her elbows to get some air to her underarms. Phillip, who was not much of a brat lately, had come to Paradise that very morning to tell her that Witherspoon had sent word that there was a letter for her, and that he didn't know whether to send it to Paradise or whether she'd be stopping at her mother's. She knew what it was. She was certain it was a response from Beadle's Dime Novels. A yes, thank you, or a no, no thank you. She could barely draw breath she was so excited and nervous and terrified. They would certainly say no as they had in the past, she'd told herself all morning, tamping down hope to prepare for the inevitable rejection.

She especially didn't want to share any of this with Adam Gentry, but she supposed she must now. He'd asked her last night to tell him about her dreams and she was obligated to, wasn't she? Well, there would be no going back now after she'd made the suggestion he come with her. Why had she done it? She'd planned to ask him for a horse to ride or the gig so that she could go to town and nothing else. What had prompted her to ask him to come along, and what had compelled him to agree?

She would wait to tell him anything until she'd read her letter. If it was a no, and it most likely was, maybe she wouldn't tell him anything at all. She certainly didn't want his pity. If it was a yes, perhaps. But it wouldn't be a yes. She was sure of it. But maybe this time . . .

Adam pulled the gig up in front of the telegraph office, jumped down, and came around to help her down, but she couldn't seem to make her legs work or take her eyes from the door, knowing that her future, well, not her entire future, but the answer to the question. of her talent, lay beyond it, folded in an envelope.

"Emmaline?" he said finally.

She turned to look at him, and he was staring at her in the strangest way. "Oh, yes. Yes." She took a deep breath and laid her hand in his.

"Would you like me to go in for you?"

Adam was looking at her with concern, as any husband might, considering she was standing in the street, unable to move her feet, or so it seemed.

She shook her head and went up the plank steps to the door of the telegraph office. She looked down at the knob, brass, she thought it might have been made of, and shiny where every customer caught it in their hand or glove and turned it to enter. She stared at the knob and the painted door, peeling and flaking down to the bare wood.

"Emmaline? Are you alright?" she heard from behind her. She nodded as she feared she was unable to do more than squeak a response. She turned the knob and walked inside.

Mrs. Witherspoon looked up. "Emmaline? I suppose I should call you Mrs. Gentry now but that doesn't seem right as your husband's mama has been Mrs. Gentry round these parts forever and a day."

"My brother," she began and stopped to clear her throat. "My brother said you had an envelope for me."

"I do, dear. Now let me find it. It's here somewhere." The woman rooted through stacks of papers and newspapers, causing Emmaline to stop breathing, thinking her letter, the one she'd been waiting for for six months, was misplaced.

"Ah, here it is." Mrs. Witherspoon held the letter above her head, shaking it as if it were a flag on the battlefield. She leaned down on her elbows on the counter, still holding the letter, and looked at Emmaline with a smile. "Now tell me about your wedding. I've heard practically nothing about the details other than what the minister's wife said."

Emmaline couldn't remove her eyes from the envelope, but she knew that if there was any hope of getting her hands on it, she was going to have to satisfy Mrs. Witherspoon's curiosity. "It was beautiful. Just beautiful," Emmaline said in a breathless voice, bringing Mrs. Witherspoon's face closer as she leaned farther across the counter.

"Yes?"

"Just beautiful. We are in love, of course, and I really only had eyes for Mr. Gentry. I hardly noticed anything else."

"What a fine match you've made!" Mrs. Witherspoon winked.

"I don't want to keep him waiting," she said, staring at the letter the woman was now holding against her bosom.

"Oh, yes! Here you are, dear, and congratulations."

Emmaline's hand shook as she took the letter, staring down at it, thinking perhaps there would be some outward sign of their intent. But how ridiculous! Did she think the editor would scratch, "you're a talentless buffoon" across the top? No, of course not.

"All the way from Buffalo, New York," Mrs. Witherspoon commented. "We don't get too many letters from New York."

"I have an aunt who lives there."

"Ah," she said and nodded. "That explains it."

Emmaline went out the door and down the steps, never removing her eyes from the scripted lettering of her name. One of the Mr. Beadles, as there were two of them, brothers, had looked at her writing and wrote the letter in return. She turned it over several times as if waiting for some divine providence to tell her what was inside.

"Emmaline? Is it bad news?"

"I don't know." She looked up at Adam, who was staring at her. "Will you take me back to Paradise now?"

He stared at her for some time until he slapped his leg with his hat and put it back on his head. "Of course. Let me help you up."

She decided on the way to Paradise that she would tell him either way. He'd been nothing but courteous to her, and she'd never known him to be spiteful or malicious. Of course, he was neither of those two things. This was Adam Gentry. A gentleman.

Someone from the stables led the gig away and Adam followed her into the house.

"I'll check back on you later," he said. "I'm sure you'll want some privacy to read your letter."

"I will"—she stopped him with her response as he turned to the door—"but I'd like to talk to you about it once I'm done reading." She held up the envelope between them. "Much of my dream lies inside."

"I'll wait here then, in the hallway."

She took a deep breath and went into the main room, closing the door behind her. She stood at the window for a minute or two thinking about what it would mean for her marriage and life if the letter contained a yes or if it contained a no. Finally, she opened the envelope with shaking fingers and pulled out a single sheet of paper that had been folded in half.

Dear Miss Somerset,

Beadle's Dime Novels would like to publish your work, Andrew Bartholomew Pans for Gold. We will publish the first five chapters one month and the next five the following. Will there be additional chapters?

Sincerely,

Erastus Beadle

She couldn't breathe. She couldn't . . . oh, dear Lord. They were going to take her book! "Adam!" she shouted. "Adam!"

"What is it, Emmaline?" He hurried to her and put his hands on her shoulders. "What is it?"

"Oh, Adam," she said and laid her hands on his chest. "It's not bad news. It's good news. Spectacular news, in fact."

"Tell me." He closed his eyes and let out a held breath. He took her hands in his.

"I'm so sorry! I've worried you, didn't I?" She smiled at him.

"You did have me worried but now that I know the news is good, I'm just curious and happy for you because I can see that whatever it is, it means a great deal to you." He kissed her knuckles.

She burst into noisy and unflattering tears. "Oh, Adam," she said finally when she could speak again. "My story is going to be published. I have been writing stories since I was very young. This is the third time I've sent something to Beadle's and I'd convinced myself that if they said no this time, I would give up. Stop writing. But they didn't say no. They said yes!"

She flung herself into his arms and he lifted her off of her feet, swinging her around in a circle. She kissed him on the mouth with a loud smack, staring into his eyes. He was smiling, crookedly, making himself look more attractive and virile than usual if that was at all possible. She dropped her eyes to his mouth. She slid down his front until her feet touched the floor, his head following hers down. He kissed her softly.

He held her face between two hands. "You write books? You never fail to surprise me, Emmaline. What will you write of our story?"

"We don't know yet, do we, Adam?" She covered his hands with her own.

"I'm just starting to think about what you've said. Beadle's? You will be writing dime novels? You *have* written a dime novel?"

She was uncertain, suddenly, about what he would think. Would she look ridiculous to him? Would he insist she quit writing and be a real wife? "I've written dime novels. *Andrew Bartholomew Pans for Gold* is the name of the one they are to publish in two parts. I've written two others that they didn't take and some stories for a magazine called *Ladies Quest*."

Adam was shaking his head, staring at her. He moved his hands to her shoulders. "You've written novels? And been published in a magazine?"

She straightened her spine. "I have."

"This is your dream? This is what you were working on last night when I found you at that desk?"

"I'm working on something new for Beadle's right now. That's what I was working on when you found me." She looked up at his face anxiously. She couldn't discern what he thought other than complete and total surprise, which was a bit of an insult if she thought about it overly long.

"I am amazed by you. I'm humbled," he said finally, releasing her shoulders and walking away. "*This* is your dream."

"Yes. This is my dream. Well, part of it anyway."

He turned back to her. "Part of it?"

"There is a place in Philadelphia, a school, a home, actually, for female writers. I want to go there," she said breathlessly. "There's a six-month course I've been accepted for." She'd never said it all out loud. Never actually put into words what her greatest wish was, but if there was ever a time to do so, it was now. Maybe it would ease the way for Adam to understand that a separation was the best possible answer for them. "I've always wanted to go there."

"Then you should go. You should chase this dream of yours."

"You will allow a divorce then?"

He shook his head and walked to her, until he was just an inch away. He gazed over her face, lingering on her mouth. "Why a divorce? This marriage of ours will be what we make of it, and I say we can make something grand. Something worthy of the Gentry expectations and the Somerset ambitions. What do you say, wife?"

He was actually going to allow her to go? Perhaps even encourage her? This was more than she'd dreamed of, more than she would allow herself to hope for. And he'd called her wife, while looking at her lips, making her take a short breath and acknowledge a shiver of awareness between her legs. It was possible she'd met her match. She wanted to throw her arms around him and make him kiss her like he'd done the day before in the hallway. She looked up at him instead.

"Who will keep house for you? Who will supervise the staff? Who will plan meals? Who will do all the things your mother has always done?"

"I'm not sure"—he closed the distance between her mouth and his—"but I can't imagine that Jenny and Mabel can't keep the house clean and cook for me. It will only be me after all."

She could feel the heat of his breath and smell hay and dirt on his clothes. "You would allow it, but would you be happy?" she whispered and glanced at his mouth.

"I think," he said and touched his lips to hers, "I think that if you are happy, then so will I be. I want this dream for you and I don't want to lose you." He kissed the side of her mouth. "You won't be gone forever, although I think I will miss you very much and probably worry myself sick over your safety."

"Will you?" She closed her eyes.

He nodded slowly, barely leaving his connection to her lips. "Will you miss me?"

Her eyes flashed open. "Yes. I find it strange considering we barely know each other but, yes. I will miss you."

He touched the seam of her lips with his tongue, tracing his way around her mouth, setting her on fire as he'd done before. His tongue touched hers and she closed her mouth and drew on it, eliciting a moan from deep in his chest. She put her hands around his neck and ran her fingers into his hair, twisting his curls as he turned his mouth to deepen their kiss and pull her against him, chest to breast and knee to knee. She was certain she would miss him.

CHAPTER 9

Adam was shocked, and that was an understatement, he thought to himself. He'd known her dreams had something to do with her neatly stacked pages of paper on the end of the secretary desk and even the ones scattered around on the floor. But it hadn't occurred to him that the young, seemingly broken, and uncomplicated young woman that he married wrote novels. His wife was an author. He felt as if he was ten foot tall! She was his wife! He'd known she was bright with a quick, sharp wit, but there was more to the process, he was certain, than just writing words and making a few jokes among them. She wrote entire novels with beginnings and middles and ends.

He pulled up from the fast pace he'd set York to and settled the horse into a walk as they made their way through some dense trees. The woods were quiet and the path thin, but he was glad Emmaline had shooed him out the door, so she could write back to Mr. Beadle. This part of the Paradise property was always where he'd come when he needed to think and be contemplative, although he hadn't been here since Josephine had died. Where he'd hidden the Morgans, the full-blooded ones his parents bought to breed, from the Confederates and the Yankees, too, during the War between the States, for months at a time, with just an occasional visit from his father or from Ben, the stable master at the time.

Adam felt certain he'd made the right decision when he'd encouraged Emmaline to attend this school, although admittedly, he'd be anything but comfortable imagining her in a big city, alone. Perhaps he should go with her, rent a house, but then who would manage Paradise? Matthew could of course, but other than foaling they would soon be in the busiest season, when they trained their horses to the bit and bridle and saddle, and sometimes, even a harness. Livie would be able to help if she weren't expecting, but she was, and he wouldn't have her do that exhausting work in her condition, and Jim would likely not allow it. He couldn't leave right now.

He'd nearly stopped Olivia's plans to live on her own and work in Washington last year, and what a catastrophe that would have been if he had. She would have resented him and maybe never recognized her love for Jim. But it had been difficult to restrain himself as the head of the family. The welfare of the women and children in his sphere was at the forefront of everything that he did and thought and planned. It had always been that way for his father and he'd lectured his sons regularly about their duty to safeguard their women, both from danger and unhappiness. Beauregard Gentry had set out to make sure that his wife was safe and comfortable and that his children were, too, and succeeded spectacularly beyond his rough-and-tumble upbringing.

He would have to admit, though, that much of Beauregard's worries stemmed from the fact that he'd saved Mother with his knife and his pistol from being sold to bandits for a twenty-dollar gold piece. Sold! His mother! Sometimes he couldn't believe the story even though it had been told to him many times, and even with all the passing years, its elements were never changed or blurred. His father had killed four men, carried mother to an abandoned cabin, allowed her to heal, and followed her, unbeknownst to her, of course, to the church in Winchester where her intended groom had rejected her. Beauregard had married her two days later. No wonder Father was so adamant. Maybe the city wouldn't be as dangerous as he imagined. Certainly, there were policemen in Philadelphia rather than just a lone sheriff, as there was here in Winchester. He wondered if he would sleep a wink while she was gone.

* * *

EMMALINE STOPPED AT JIM AND OLIVIA'S HOUSE AFTER GOING back to Winchester to send her letter to Mr. Beadle and send her telegraph to Clair House, home of the studies for women authors. She was hoping they would take her on.

"You must never bother knocking," Olivia said as she pulled her inside. "You're family. And you're looking well, with some color to your cheeks and a spring in your step."

Emmaline smiled and hugged her sister-in-law. She was perfect for her quiet giant of a brother. "I have come to ask a favor and am hoping you have something cold to drink. I'm parched!"

Olivia pulled her along toward the kitchen. "I have cold tea, and I made a fruitcake that is barely edible unless you add mounds of butter."

"Your house is looking wonderful," Emmaline said as they went down the short hallway and into the kitchen. "And you're looking healthy and happy." She looked pointedly at Olivia's slightly rounded belly.

"Oh, Emmaline! I'm so wondrously happy, I don't know what do with myself! I'm so looking forward to this baby." She set out two glasses and pulled a pitcher of tea from the icebox. "I've never been much of seamstress, but I've made some of the most darling clothes, and Mother ships me things from all the fashionable stores in Washington."

Olivia hurried out of the room and came back holding up a tiny nightgown, its edges embroidered with yellow and green thread. She handed it to Emmaline. "I've done all the sewing myself!"

Emmaline took the garment from her, fingered the fabric, and examined the small stitches around the scalloped hem as she dropped down onto a kitchen chair. She didn't realize she was crying until a tear fell on her hand. And then her tears came in torrents, hiccoughing sobs, making her nose run and her eyes blur.

"Oh no," Olivia said and knelt in front of her. "How thoughtless of me. How absolutely cruel. I am so sorry to go on and on about it."

Emmaline shook her head and blew her nose. "You must not stop. I am very glad for you and Jim both."

Olivia sat down beside her and picked up her hand. "I'm so sorry, Emmaline."

"I never was excited about it, you know, not like you. I didn't feel well, and the circumstances were dreadful." She looked up at her sister-in-law then, tears tumbling again down her cheeks. "I feel so guilty now that he's lost that I wasn't more excited about his birth. I didn't get to see him either, you know. But that would have been worse, I think, in some ways."

"I was there. I lined the box they buried him in," Olivia said and wiped tears from her own eyes. "I doubt if you remember me being there much that first week, but I was there with your mother and sisters. I don't believe you have anything to feel guilty about. You grieved deeply, Emmaline. Perhaps you don't remember. You'd lost quite a bit of blood."

"That week isn't clear in my memory, but I wonder if that's just the nature of loss. Maybe we don't remember what we can't manage. Your mother sent me letters that were a comfort, and

Annie visited several times. Adam was very sad, too, although, it's strange, is it not, that he might have considered it a relief but didn't."

"It's not strange at all. Adam is the best of men, other than Jim, of course."

"He is. He's done something so remarkable for me that I can barely believe it. But this isn't what I've come to talk to you about. You must be very busy."

"Please tell me, Emmaline. What has Adam done? Excuse me, but I'm desperate to hear how the two of you are doing after your loss. So is your mother and Nettie and Jane and Betsy, although Betsy is so excited about her wedding, she can't sit still."

"I'm not surprised about Betsy. She's been pining for Edwin for years." She looked up at Olivia. "I've kept everything to myself and made everyone who loves me worry, haven't I?"

"We are worried about you and about Adam, but marriages are private. I understand and so does everyone else."

"I may as well tell you." Emmaline smiled. "I'm too excited to hold it in."

Just as Emmaline began to share her story, her brother Jim arrived home and kissed her cheek and his wife's lips. "What am I interrupting?"

"You must be quiet. Emmaline has exciting news and is just about to share it with us. Oh, do sit down, dear. You're most likely tired and hungry. Would you like me to cut you a piece of fruitcake?"

Jim shook his head. "No thank you, Livie. Go ahead with your news, Emmaline."

So, she told them.

"Adam is going to allow this move to the city?" Jim said sternly when she was done.

"Adam is my husband, but he doesn't do my deciding for me. I've longed for four years to get admitted to Clair House. Just as I was preparing to tell Mother and everyone else that I was going there, I found myself expecting a baby with no husband. Adam respects me enough to be happy for me."

"I'll bet he's worried and beside himself," Jim said.

"But this is so exciting about your book!" Olivia said. "I'm so proud of you! I never knew you did any writing."

"Betsy was the only one that knew," she said. "It never seemed real enough to tell everyone else, especially after I was rejected so many times. I'm very excited, and Adam is, too."

"Of course, he is. We're all hoping that the two of you will be very happy together. Maybe even fall in love." Olivia grinned.

"I don't know about the falling in love part, but I don't think we'll be divorcing or separating. He's adamant."

"What?" Jim said loudly. "Divorcing?"

"Oh, dear," Olivia covered her mouth with her hand.

"You've got to put that out of your head, Emmaline," Jim said. "Marriage is for good. Mother would be . . ."

"You may quit lecturing me any minute. I understand the hurt and embarrassment I've caused our family, and now I've involved the Gentrys." She stood, feeling angry and betrayed. "But my feelings, my wants and needs and dreams and desires have always been less because they weren't the same as every other female's. I'm going to Philadelphia and learn more about my writing. My story will be published in Beadle's, and my husband supports me in both things."

Emmaline turned on her heel and hurried to the front door. Jim caught her by the arm and wrapped her up against his chest.

"I'm sorry," he said and kissed the top of her head. "It's just that I worry about you."

"I know. But I'm just not like the others. I'm just not."

He held her away from his chest and smiled a lopsided grin. "I'm glad you are exactly who you are. I couldn't be prouder of you and this writing. I can hardly take it in."

"Are you sure?"

He tilted his head to the side and regarded her for several long moments. "Of course, I'm sure. You were always the smartest of the bunch of us."

Olivia kissed her cheek and then patted her own belly. "This baby is going to have a famous aunt. I'm sure of it."

"I almost forgot why I stopped by. I need your help, Olivia. I'm going to Bessie's to order several new things and I'd like you to come with me. I'm going to ask Nettie to come, too. You both always manage to wear the right color and style and I'm always in a gray or brown seed sack, it seems."

"Shopping? Of course! We could go into Washington and visit Mother instead and order at all the fashionable salons the week after Betsy's wedding! What do you think? Will Nettie be able to slip away?"

"I never thought about going to Washington to shop. Would Eleanor mind, do you think?"

"Mind? Heavens no! She'd be very excited!"

Jim kissed Olivia's head. "What is this going to cost me?"

"Never you mind," she said and laughed. "I'll send a letter to Mother right away."

Emmaline walked the three blocks to Nettie's, her mind racing with what she'd said to Jim and Olivia. She was no longer considering any type of separation, it seemed, or at least that was what she'd said. Was that exactly what she believed? Or was she too busy defending herself to her brother, the dearest person in her world, and the person she was closest to, although, it was Adam she'd wanted to tell first. It was Adam she wanted to hug and kiss. It was Adam's approval, and approval wasn't quite the right word, but it was something like that. She wanted his support and respect and she'd received it. Did she want more?

Emmaline hugged and kissed her niece and nephew and drew her sister to the kitchen. She told her about Beadle's and Clair House and asked her about a visit to Washington to shop if they could convince Jane to take her children to their mother's as John was away most days.

"What did Adam say? Is he upset about you moving away to Philadelphia?"

"It's only for six months, but yes, I think he is worried. But mostly he talked about how excited he is for me."

"How are you feeling? That last time I saw you, you looked like a scarecrow. You look much better now. We've all been worried about you."

"I'm better. I'm finally feeling myself."

"There'll be other children," Nettie said and hugged herself. "I've been hoping for a third myself."

"Well . . . there may be other children, but we haven't done what was necessary to produce one yet." Emmaline looked at her sister. "I have questions."

"Are you not feeling up to it?"

"I'm feeling very much up to it, but there are some complications."

"Is he not feeling up to it?" Nettie asked, a look of horror on her face. "John said that can happen to a man as he gets older."

"Adam isn't old! He's only a few years older than John and Matt and Jim."

"Why haven't you, you know, done what was necessary, then?"

Emmaline dropped into one of the kitchen chairs. "I would like to and I'm fairly certain he would like to. We've done some . . . touching." She looked up at her sister. "But if I am to attend Clair House, I cannot be with child again."

"There are ways to prevent babies, you know," Nettie said as she stirred a pot on the stove and peeked through the doorway to where the children were playing with a puzzle.

"What are they?"

Nettie shrugged. "For a time, right after Albert, John would . . . end things on my stomach instead of inside me."

"So, the seed was not . . ."

"Planted."

"There are other ways?"

"There are always sheaths," she said and stared sightlessly out her kitchen window. "John thinks they're more reliable than the other."

"I wouldn't know where to . . ."

"That is for Adam to worry about. Tell him you would like to continue the touching to its conclusion but don't want to become pregnant. He'll know what to do."

But that wasn't the entire problem, was it. It wasn't so much about obtaining sheaths, although she'd have no idea how to do it, it was about consummating the marriage, making it impossible to wiggle out of, she imagined. Without the complete act . . . she was still free. Or was she?

"Once we get to this conclusion, I'll be his wife in earnest," she whispered. "There'll be no turning back." And she wondered if he would ever be happy with her. She watched him from the corner of her eye in the evenings when she was finishing her writing and he was reading a book or the newspaper. But that was just it. Often, he wasn't reading, just holding a book and staring into the fireplace or out the window. She felt certain he was thinking about Josephine. He was still grieving, and she wondered if he'd ever recover.

Nettie pulled bread from the oven and the children came running. She sliced the warm loaf, added butter and jam, and handed each child a piece. They went out the back door to sit on the porch. She turned to her sister, hands on her hips. "You're already his wife in earnest whether you wish to believe it or not. There never was an opportunity to turn back other than prior to your wedding. You can make your life miserable or you can make the best of it. Adam Gentry is handsome, wealthy, and apparently thrilled that his wife writes novels. What else do you want?"

"I'm not sure," she said. "The Gentrys are rich, true, and he was honestly excited about my writing. He is attractive, too. Very much so."

"Then what are you waiting for, Emmaline?" Nettie asked with some exasperation. "Be his wife in every way. Find out how your marriage is going to work. Talk to him. Especially right after you've made love—John is very pliable afterwards—and you may be able to set up a routine that is mostly to your liking."

"Is that what you do?"

"Of course!"

"But you love John and he you. It's sickening sometimes to watch you two."

Nettie sighed and shrugged her shoulders, a little smile on her lips and a faraway look in her eye. "Yes. Yes, we do love each other." She turned back to the oven and moved the coffeepot to boil. "Maybe you will love Adam in the same way, Emmaline. You're not as immune to soft feelings as you make yourself out to be."

EMMALINE HAD BEEN QUIET AT DINNER AND SAT AT THE DESK IN the main room, equally writing on paper and crumbling it into balls. He opened a book, propped his legs on the leather hassock, and tried to relax but his eyes continued to drift toward her. Her posture was rigid, and her face focused and serious. His bride took her writing to heart. He was going to ask her one of these days to allow him to read something she'd written, but he wasn't sure she was ready to share with him. He sensed her writing was intensely personal, and they were not yet intimates. She turned to him as she tried to fix her fountain pen and only managed to squirt ink on her blouse. She dabbed at it and looked up at him.

"I don't know quite how to ask you this," she said.

"Ask me anything you want."

"I went to see Olivia and Nettie to ask them to come with me to Bessie's and help me pick out some new things to wear. I'd like to arrive in Philadelphia looking more put together and stylish than I usually do, although I don't understand why. I've never given one damn about my clothing before."

He chuckled. "Maybe it's because you've been looking forward to this for a long time and want to make a good impression."

"You're right, of course. I am vain in the extreme."

He laughed outright. "There's nothing the matter with wanting to look your best, although you are a very beautiful woman regardless of what you're wearing."

She blushed, her face and neck turning pink. He watched the color recede below the edge of her dress. "Well. That is ridiculous."

"What is it you wished to talk about, Emmaline?" he asked after several minutes had gone by.

"Olivia said we should take the train to Washington and visit your mother and go to all the shops there if Jane will manage Nettie's children for a few days."

"Mother would be thrilled to see all of you. What's the problem, then?"

"I have enough money saved for the tuition at Clair House and a bit extra but I'm thinking that the shops in Washington will be much more expensive than Bessie's." She stopped abruptly and stared at him. "Do you think you could lend me some money until I'm paid by Beadle's?"

"Lend you some money?"

"I promise to pay it back as soon—"

"Emmaline. You are *not* borrowing any money from me. You're my wife. I've already set up an account at the bank here in town with money for your personal use. I will have to ask Mother what the most convenient way would be to take care of the bills at the shops in Washington. She probably has credit accounts set up at the shops she frequents, so it may just be a matter of her forwarding the bills to me."

She laid her pen down on the desk and stared at him. "You've opened a bank account for me?' she whispered.

"There is one thousand dollars available to you at any time, although when you're shopping in Winchester, just add what you spend to the Paradise account as we have one set up at nearly every merchant."

"One thousand dollars?"

He nodded. "I've been meaning to talk to you about your time in Philadelphia, too. You'll have to tell me where I'll be sending the tuition, and if you can find a bank that is reputable and close to the school, I'll set up an account there for you. You'll have to have funds to live on."

"You're going to pay my tuition?"

"Yes. Of course, I am. You're a Gentry now and your expenses will be paid for with Gentry money. And do not, I repeat, do not purchase one blouse and one skirt for yourself. You are in need of a new wardrobe. Get everything necessary and don't forget to get a coat for next winter while you're there. Shall I write Mother and tell her to make sure you have purchased everything you need?"

She shook her head. "I'm to have a new wardrobe?"

Adam stood and walked to her. "I don't want to be unkind, but I've seen the clothing you've hung in our rooms. There are two skirts, one brown, one gray, a few blouses, none of which do not have ink stains, a dress I've seen you in at church, and the dress you were married in. That's all."

Emmaline groaned. "Please don't repeat what you've said to my mother. She was furious with me because I would never purchase anything at Bessie's. My sisters would be so excited they couldn't sleep before they ordered new things, and I managed to make myself scarce to avoid it. She didn't say, but Mother was embarrassed at what I brought here in my suitcase. She wanted to burn it all."

Adam took her hand and drew her to her feet. They were standing just a few inches apart and he put his hands on her waist, enjoying the feel of it and remembering her in their bed the day before.

"You must have new skirts and blouses, dresses, and jackets." He stepped closer and laid a hand on her cheek. "And don't forget the silk stockings, embroidered chemises, lace drawers, and filmy night things," he whispered.

She looked up at him from under her lashes, her lips parting. "I was thinking," she said softly.

He touched his lips to her eyes and her cheeks. "What were you thinking?"

She laid her hands on his chest and let them drift up until she touched bare skin at his open collar, wrapping her fingers around his neck and touching his ears with her thumbs. He groaned.

"I've been thinking that, well, I would like to continue from where we began yesterday"—she touched his cheek, dragging her hand over the dark beard that was already beginning to show—"but . . ."

He turned his face into her hand and kissed her palm and tried to contain his arousal. "But . . . what?"

She looked in his eyes then, worried, and maybe nervous, and he thought he might move a mountain, as trite as the saying was, to erase her troubles. It felt as though he *was* meant to be with her and she with him. It felt right.

"I don't want to be expecting a child right this moment. I want to go to Clair House. I want to focus on my writing. If my first pregnancy was anything to go by, I don't want to be sick for months at a time right now, although, when the time was right, I think I'd make whatever sacrifice was necessary. There are ways to prevent babies, aren't there?"

He nodded and moved to whisper in her ear and ran his tongue around the shell of it, eliciting a deep breath from her. "There are ways."

"Nettie said to ask you about sheaths and—"

"Your sister is a fountain of knowledge, is she not," he interrupted and brought his hand to the back of her neck, pulling her forward until her lips touched his. She kissed him back, tracing his mouth with her tongue. Her lips were soft and warm and unschooled. But yet, she was passionate, he knew. "Let me worry about this. It's my responsibility to make sure you're happy and comfortable. And satisfied."

"Satisfied," she whispered and opened her eyes.

He touched his mouth to hers. "Are you ready to retire, Mrs. Gentry?"

"Should we bank the fire and lower the lamps?" she asked as she brushed her lips back and forth across his.

He stepped away from her, lacing his fingers with hers as he did, pulling her gently to follow him. "Let Jenny get them."

Emmaline went directly to the bathing chamber while he rummaged through the valise in the back of his dressing room. He found the sheaths that he'd quit using with Josephine, knowing their child was already conceived, and put them on his nightstand. He pulled off his clothes and scrambled under the sheets, prepared to wait for his bride. God, he was nervous.

The door opened, and she walked to the bed, staring at him, wearing her knee-length nightgown that had haunted his dreams. She stopped, reached down, and pulled the nightgown over her head, leaving her naked, one knee on the edge of the mattress. He couldn't breathe. His heart was pounding in his chest, and he was certain she heard him moan.

"I imagine you wanted to see me as much as I want to see you."

He growled and threw back the sheet, exposing himself, staring at her, letting his eyes wander to her breasts, full, dark tips hardening under his watch. Her belly was flat, leading to flared, rounded hips framing a dark patch of hair. He looked up and found her staring at his cock. He was fully, and even painfully aroused.

"Come here, wife."

Her lashes lowered as she knelt on the bed and came to him on her hands and knees. He could barely restrain himself from reaching out to touch her breasts as they swayed back and forth with her movement. She crawled over him, stretching out like a cat, her toes touching his shins, her breasts flattened on his chest, as she leaned her forearms on his shoulders, her hair dropping around his face, smelling like soap and like Emmaline. She pulled forward and his cock popped up between her thighs.

"Umm," she said and smiled.

"Umm is right." He brought his hands to her ass, rocking her hips against him.

She dropped her eyes, staring at her hands, and whispered, "Mother always said I was too forward about . . . earthy matters. I haven't been demure, have I?"

He captured her face in his hands and gently tilted it up until she was looking at him. "You have been perfect. We're man and wife. We're in this bed to pleasure each other and to someday make our children. You're safe here with me to do and act as naturally as you want." He kissed her openmouthed and spoke again just a hairsbreadth from her lips. "The openness of your desires heightens mine. I want you, Emmaline Gentry. I want to be inside you."

She sat back on her heels while he opened the wrapping on the sheath with shaking fingers. He pulled it down around his cock as she watched and licked her lips. She stretched out on him again, rubbing her breasts against him and kissing him, tangling her tongue with his.

They were both breathing heavily when he flipped her onto her back and reached down with his hand to pull her leg up and around his hip. He touched her intimately and licked her breasts, sucking hard on her nipples until her back arched and he could feel her inner muscles clenching on his fingers.

He put his cock at her entrance, wiggling inside just a bit, and looked her in the eyes. "I don't know if you'll have any pain, Emmaline," he said and kissed her. "I surely hope not." His shoulders shook with desire and need, his muscles bunched under her fingers as she trailed her hand up his forearms, her eyes half-mast and her lips parted. She thrust her hips up in one smooth, swift motion, bringing him inside her as far as he could go. They both moaned, and his hips began to pump against her. She tossed her head from side to side, stopped to stare at him, and then tilted her head back, exposing the long column of her throat as her eyes fluttered and she went limp under him.

CHAPTER 10

Emmaline was still awake when she heard the hallway clock chime two in the morning. Adam had fallen asleep nearly as soon as he'd rolled off of her. She was propped up on her elbow, chin on her hand, watching him sleep in the moonlight that poured in the window across from their bed. He was beautiful and masculine even in sleep, and it made her aware of herself with tremors between her legs. She could hardly believe that he'd touched her with his hands and mouth and put himself in her. She would have never thought of him as desirable or sexual. Honorable, yes. Handsome, yes. But not this overwhelming need to touch him *everywhere*. She would miss this. She would miss him, she realized again.

His arm was laid on the pillow above his head and his breathing was deep and even. She ran her finger lightly up through the hair on his chest, to his shoulder, through the soft hair under his arm, and over the underside of his bicep, hard and wide. Like other parts of him, Emmaline said to herself and smiled secretively. She wasn't certain she wanted to let him out of her sight. Her fingers reversed course, a feather touch, following his chest hair as it tapered away under the sheet he'd pulled up to his waist. She glanced further and saw that he was beginning to be aroused. She licked her lips and looked up at him. His eyes were still closed.

"When you stare at it . . ." he said and took a deep breath as she reached her hand under the sheet.

"Your eyes are closed. How do you know I was staring at it?"

"Because I know." Adam opened his eyes and rolled onto his side, facing her. He ran his knuckle down her cheek and pushed his fingers through her hair. "Are you sore from our love making? Did I hurt you?"

She shook her head. "No. You didn't hurt me, although you fell asleep before I could ask you anything and Nettie said that John is the most pliable and forthcoming right after . . ."

Adam laughed, a low, rich sound that reverberated through her and made her smile. "I've known John Winders since we were both boys and I don't imagine he'd like me knowing that bit of his marriage."

"You must never let on!"

He kissed her nose. "No. I suppose I shouldn't. What would I say anyway?"

Emmaline smiled and giggled and dropped her voice an octave. "'I hear you're an easy mark after your wife has had her way with you!'"

He laughed again and looked at her. "Is there something you wanted to ask me about when I so unceremoniously fell asleep? I'm an old man and need my rest. Are you sure I didn't hurt you?"

"I wasn't a virgin, you know."

"I know," he whispered in her ear. "We both knew when we married that neither of us were virgins."

"But in some ways, I was. I wanted to thank you for being so thoughtful and making me feel so wanted." She felt the shimmer of tears in her eyes.

He kissed her softly. "You are *very* enticing. There was no effort to make you feel wanted. I wanted you. I'm thinking that your first experience wasn't to your liking and I'm hoping I've erased every unpleasant memory, if I'm right."

"You are right. I didn't not even realize it was happening at first." She felt her lip tremble. "I was such a fool, thinking about it now, especially now, knowing how wonderful it could be."

"Don't ever call or think of yourself as a fool. You were innocent, and he took advantage, surely one of the worst things a person can do to another." He rolled onto his back staring at the ceiling. He turned his head to look at her then. "You thought it wonderful?"

She nodded. "Beyond my wildest expectation."

His mouth hitched to one side and then flattened into a line. "I would like to find him and send him to perdition."

"You sound very fierce."

"About him? Yes," he said and leaned over her until she lay flat on her back. "I think I'll be fierce about anything or anyone that bothers you until we are both resting in our graves."

She tangled her feet with his, and he lifted her breast in his hand in a casual possession that left her breathless. He pulled a sheath over himself and moved over her, spreading her legs as he did, entering her in one motion. She was wet already and she could hear the slow, rhythmic in and out of their lovemaking. His face was beside hers, buried in her hair, and she could feel his damp breathing against her ear, hitching pants that increased in tempo with every thrust. She pulled her knees up, feet flat, on either side of his legs, laid her hands on his flanks, and closed her eyes. She and he were, at that moment, the very definition of intimate, locked together, both feeling the gradual build of intense arousal, naked against each other, and he in her very body. She arched against him and her knees and hands fell to her side, limp and sweat-soaked.

"Jesus, Emmaline," he whispered as he pumped in her hard and fast. Growling and shaking and twitching when she touched his back as he released and dropped his weight on her. Her eyes closed shortly after.

Emmaline awoke the next morning and found herself alone in their bed, although she could hear her husband running water into the bathing tub and humming a tune. Last night, her wedding night in earnest, was a revelation. There could be passion and awareness and humor and anticipation between husbands and wives, culminating in an act so divine, she couldn't find words to describe it satisfactorily. No wonder Nettie couldn't keep her hands off of her husband. She did this with John! But Nettie was in love. She surely was not. She liked Adam. She would admit he'd saved her from an uncomfortable future and had been kind and thoughtful more than she could have anticipated, but still she wouldn't describe him as being in love and she certainly was not in love with him. How ridiculous!

"GIRLS! OVER HERE! OLIVIA!" EMMALINE HEARD AS SHE STOOD on the top step of the stopped train at the Washington station, waiting for her sister and Olivia to step down. She followed them through the throngs of people crowding the platform until they got to Mrs. Gentry.

Eleanor was hugging Olivia then, swaying back and forth and kissing her cheeks and hair. "Oh, how I've missed you!" she said as Olivia burst into tears.

"I'm sorry"—Olivia kissed her mother's cheek—"I cry all the time it seems!"

Eleanor kissed Emmaline and then insisted on kissing Nettie, too. "Come, girls. We will make some introductions in the carriage."

"This lovely lady is Fiona McKellar," Eleanor said when they were on their way at a brisk clip. "Fiona, you've met Olivia. This is my daughter-in-law, Emmaline, Adam's wife, and this is her sister Nettie."

"It is good to see you again, ma'am," Olivia said. "Mother seems so happy in her letters and I think it must be because of your hospitality."

"How sweet of you!" Fiona said. "Eleanor and I have been having a grand time. We're enjoying ourselves immensely, and your mother is quite sought out when we attend garden parties and soirees."

"I told my brothers that she was a very popular lady at social events," Olivia said, smiling and leaning forward to pat her mother's knee.

"Ah, here we are, ladies," Miss McKellar said as the carriage pulled onto a graveled drive in front of a huge brick home, three stories tall. The front door opened, and a middle-aged woman dressed in pale gray and a starched white apron stepped out. "That is Mrs. Hodgkins, my housekeeper. She is a dear and will make sure you are comfortable."

Emmaline was shown to a spacious bedroom with a private bathing chamber. A young woman was hanging her clothes and told her to ring the bell near the bed if she needed assistance. The room was beautifully and expensively decorated, she knew, even if she'd never paid much attention to such things. She washed her face and hands, tucked her hair back into the bun at the base of her neck, and stared at herself in the mirror hanging there. It was probably time to start acting a bit more like an adult woman and presenting herself as one. She needn't be excessive with styling her hair and what clothes she wore but she knew that her flippant disorder, meant as much to confound her mother as it was to please herself, should be put to rest. She was about to be a published author, heading to an exclusive writing school soon, and Adam Gentry's wife. Adam Gentry's wife in every way.

She smiled to herself then, thinking about the night before she boarded the train when Adam had climbed into the bathing tub with her, scrubbing her and soaping her skin until she was writhing in his hands and the tiled floor of the bathing room was wet from the water sloshing out of the tub. That very morning he'd helped her into the carriage, stopped for Olivia and Nettie, and taken them all to the train station. He managed their luggage, kissed his sister on the cheek, and handed each of them up the stairs to the conductor. But before she'd taken the step, he'd wrapped his hand around the back of her neck and kissed her on the mouth. Right there at the station, in front of everyone. Well.

Emmaline left her room before she could think any more on that and went down the long stairway of the house, hearing feminine laughter coming from an open doorway down a wide, carpeted hallway. She found her sister, Miss McKellar, and her mother-in-law seated together in a cozy grouping of couches and chairs, all covered in a wide green and white stripe fabric, in front of three long windows draped in a green, white, and pink floral design.

"Come sit with us and enjoy a lemonade, Emmaline," Eleanor said. "Olivia is napping."

"Yes, thank you," she said and seated herself where Eleanor was patting the seat on the sofa beside her.

"You must tell us everything now. I want to hear every single thing about your writing and, of course, about Adam, too," Eleanor said and laughed, beaming at Emmaline.

"Your mother-in-law couldn't contain herself, dear, after reading the letters from your husband." Miss McKellar handed Emmaline a frosted glass of lemonade. "Writers are such interesting people."

Emmaline looked from one woman to the other, feeling odd about their enthusiasm, although *odd* wasn't the right word. Certainly, it was fine for her to feel excitement and victorious about being accepted for Beadle's, but she didn't anticipate others feeling the same or even complimenting her. Eleanor turned in her seat to face her and reached for her hand. But this was

Eleanor Gentry, who she knew didn't have a single devious bone in her body.

"Oh, don't be coy, Emmaline," Nettie said when a few quiet moments had passed. "Everyone is very excited for you, you've just always believed that no one noticed your existence. This is a great accomplishment."

Emmaline swallowed. "I . . . I . . ."

"Adam has written me several letters about the day you found out that your story would be published. He is so proud of you," Eleanor said and squeezed her hand. "But I would like to hear the story from you, please. Tell me about the day that you found out and about how you decided to become a writer."

Emmaline felt a curious tightening of her throat and stared at her hands. He was proud of her? She dared not look at Eleanor for fear of voicing all the frustrations and all the fears and all the doubts that she'd carried with her for what seemed like forever. "Adam wrote you letters about my books?" she asked quietly without lifting her head.

Eleanor scooted closer. She touched Emmaline's cheek, bringing her face up, and waited until Emmaline looked into her eyes. "He did. I haven't heard him talk joyously about anything since . . . well, for quite some time. He thinks you must be exceptionally clever and is hoping one day you'll allow him to read some of your stories. For now, he's patiently, or impatiently waiting for the edition of Beadle's that includes *Andrew Bartholomew Pans for Gold.*"

Emmaline took slow, deep breaths, hoping to settle her heartbeat. She glanced at Nettie, who raised her brows, as if to say, *I told you so*, and allowing Emmaline to get past the lure of tears and self-pity.

"I started writing down stories as soon as I was able to write, maybe when I was eight or nine years old. I stole paper from my father's desk until I'd used all of his and he caught me one day sneaking out of his office. He asked me what I was doing with it, and I told him I was writing a story about a family who lived in a small town and whose children were forever getting into trouble. I told him the mother was a bit silly but lovable nonetheless and that the father was perfect in every way."

Nettie laughed. "You didn't say that to him!"

"I did." Emmaline smiled at her sister. "He kissed my head and told me to keep writing, that I mustn't make the father too perfect because it wouldn't be believable. He told me I was going to be . . . I was going to do . . ." But she couldn't finish for the foolish tears. "Damn it. I never cry."

Nettie's lip was trembling. "Of course, he told you that. He was the very best daddy."

"Mr. Somerset was a wonderful father and husband, and a dear friend to the Gentry family. I think he would be exceptionally pleased that we are related now twice over," Eleanor said.

"But you haven't told us, dear, about the day you received the letter," Fiona said kindly, clearly trying to lighten the mood.

Emmaline recounted the day, embellishing the story a bit to draw some laughter. "And then I called to Adam to come into the room and he picked me up and spun me around. He wasn't even sure what the news was, and yet he was so happy for me, even when I told him I wanted to go to the Clair School in Philadelphia. That's when I started thinking that my chance to go there was actually real and that I would show up on the doorstep wearing a frayed gray skirt, mended drawers, and an ink-stained blouse. I decided I must have some new things and knew I wasn't qualified to choose them."

Eleanor laughed and hugged her. "You have come to the right place. Washington has a number of fashionable dressmakers. We'll visit at least two of them and see which one suits your style."

"I don't know what my style is," Emmaline said.

"We'll find out, though, and we have several other exciting things planned for you all," Fiona said. "We're going to have such fun!"

* * *

"WHAT DO YOU THINK OF THIS FABRIC, MOTHER?" OLIVIA asked the following morning as they browsed at Mrs. Finch's Dress Shop and Millinery.

"It's lovely. Are you thinking of a dress for yourself?"

"I'll need a few things for church that will fit me for the next few months and thought I'd place an order while I was here. There are so many beautiful and different fabrics. Bessie is making me some everyday skirts and dresses."

Nettie was already speaking to a young woman and holding a shiny burgundy silk up to her neck as she looked at herself in a full-length mirror. Emmaline didn't know where to begin.

Eleanor caught her by the arm and escorted her to a glass counter at the back of the store. "Ah, Mrs. Finch," she said when a petite blonde came through the curtain. "My daughter-in-law needs a new wardrobe and I'm hoping you can help us. And we'll need a few ready to purchase items as well."

"Certainly," Mrs. Finch said and came out from behind the counter, turning Emmaline this way and then that. "Come. Let's take your measurements and then I will show you and your mother-in-law what options you have, and you can tell me what you like and don't like and what your everyday habits are."

Soon, Emmaline was standing on a platform in front of several mirrors in her chemise and drawers with Eleanor in a chair off to the side of the room. Mrs. Finch took one look at Emmaline's underthings and sent a young girl into a storeroom.

"Well, you've got the figure to wear just about anything," Mrs. Finch said. "Tell me about what you do regularly."

"I sit at a desk and write. I do little cooking, thankfully no cleaning, although I've only been married for a short while. I imagine there'll be times of the year I'll need to help the staff with large jobs," Emmaline said and looked at Eleanor, who nodded.

"So, you're not doing morning calls or receiving in the afternoon, then. Do you and your husband plan to entertain much?"

Emmaline shrugged. "I don't dress to receive callers if that's what you mean, and I really don't know if Adam intends to entertain much or not. I'll be away in Philadelphia for six months soon."

The young woman returned and handed Emmaline silk underthings and took the ones she was wearing from her hand after she'd changed behind a paneled screen. The fabric slid over her skin and was feminine with some lace at the neckline and the edges of the legs.

"I think you will need three day dresses, at least six or eight skirts and blouses, two dressier dresses, and the gloves, hats, and jackets to match."

"She'll also need a winter coat suitable for church or visiting, and I think we'd be wise to order at least ten skirts and blouses, perhaps some vests and shawls, too."

"All the undergarments, of course," Mrs. Finch said.

"And filmy night clothes," Emmaline said as Olivia, Nettie, and Fiona came into the dressing room. "My husband told me to buy silk stockings and filmy night things."

Olivia covered her mouth with her hand, and Nettie's eyes widened.

Eleanor Gentry cleared her throat. "Yes, dear. You really didn't have a trousseau, did you?"

"A full selection of bedroom attire then?" Mrs. Finch asked.

Emmaline swallowed. "I guess so."

"Let me show you some ready-made dresses that you can take home now or later today if there are alterations to be done," the dressmaker said.

* * *

"Come in," Emmaline said to a knock at the door of her sleeping room the following morning.

Olivia and Nettie came through quickly and closed the door behind them. "You're almost dressed," Nettie said.

"A message has come from Mrs. Finch. The alterations are done on some of your ready-to-wear items," Olivia said. "We thought the three of us could go ourselves, without Mother and Miss McKellar."

"There's no need to bother them," Nettie said quickly. "Hurry up and put your shoes on."

"What's the rush? I haven't eaten anything, and I'm starved."

"There are muffins in the breakfast room that look delicious. You can take one of those with you. We have already asked Miss McKellar if we may call for her coach and it's coming from the carriage house right now."

"Where is Eleanor?" Emmaline asked.

"She and Miss McKellar like to take a morning walk," Olivia said. "Mother said she's not as active here as she was at home and likes to get some exercise before the heat is oppressive."

Emmaline followed the two women, and soon they were off to Mrs. Finch's. She was looking forward to having new things, which was strange for her, but she'd been imagining knocking on the door of Clair House in one of her ink-stained blouses and now she could see herself instead in the navy twill skirt and the cream blouse with the navy trim and embroidered cuffs. Olivia and Nettie were both staring at the passing houses and people rather than chattering as they usually did.

"I received a note that a few items in my order have been finished," Emmaline said. "I'd like to pick them up now, please."

"Certainly," a young woman said. "Let me get them for you."

Mrs. Finch came through the curtain a few moments later followed by the young woman with a stack of wrapped packages and boxes. "Mr. Underwood, the shoemaker, sent this pair of half boots for you until he could complete the rest of your order. Aren't they darling?"

"They're perfect," Emmaline said after trying them on and admiring them in the mirror. "And you have the address to send the bills?"

"Mrs. Gentry has given me your Winchester address, yes. Some of your other items will be done within the next few days, hopefully before you travel home, but the bulk of the custom-made things will be shipped to the address we have for the bill. Is there anything else I can do for you today?"

"I don't think—" Emmaline began.

"I'd like to add a few items to my order," Nettie said.

"I would also," Olivia added.

"Would you ladies like to see more designs or other fabrics?"

Nettie shook her head. "No, ma'am. I'd just like to purchase some . . . bedroom attire."

"Yes. I would like to order some as well," Olivia said, a blush creeping up her neck. "I'd like to pay you in cash now, if it's suitable. I don't want my husband to receive the bill for, perhaps, two gowns with matching robes."

"I have cash money, too," Nettie said. "Do you have anything with feathers?"

CHAPTER 11

"I thought you were going to buy some new clothes while you visited Mother," Adam said as he walked into the main room and saw Emmaline with her head bent over papers, her pen flying. "Oh. I'm sorry. I'll come back when you're finished."

"No," she said. "One minute . . . just one more minute."

Adam waited patiently, watching her, glad she was home, in their house. There was something distressing about her being away, although he wouldn't share that with a soul, and he wondered if she felt the same. She laid down her pen and shrugged out of the old stained blouse she wore, and he had a visceral reaction below his waist as she did. She stood and turned to him then, in a full dark blue skirt with a small bustle, and a starched white shirt with a scoop neck and matching blue roped embroidery around the neckline and cuffs.

"Well, don't you look like a most accomplished lady," he said eyeing her from the top of her hair to the new, shiny boots sticking out from under her hem. She smoothed some imaginary wrinkles from her skirt and looked at him, waiting, he supposed. He took both her hands in his, kissing the back of them, and smiled at her. "You really are very beautiful."

She blushed and then smiled. "I think this is my favorite. Do you like it?"

"I do. I hope you bought plenty of pretty things if they make you smile like this."

"I like all my new things, although many of them will be shipped here because they weren't complete. Your mother insisted on me buying much more than I planned." She looked up at him with wide eyes. "I can't imagine how much that bill will be."

"You are my wife. It's my privilege to see your needs, and we are not beggared. Tell me about you trip."

Her face lit up with excitement. "Oh, Adam! I had such fun. I have so much to tell you. I've asked Mabel to make us a tray of lemonade and cookies on the patio so that we can sit and talk. Do you . . .?"

He kissed her then, midsentence, pulling her to him with his arms around her waist and hers hanging at her side. He'd promised himself while she was on this trip to be more spontaneous, more cheerful, more focused on her than he had been so far in their marriage. He was private about his remaining grief for Josephine, and for the child they'd lost, but it hung on him he knew, and even though he'd pushed it aside to engage her in conversation, he thought she knew there was a cloud above him sometimes. Knew that sometimes when he read the same page over and again as they sat beside each other in the evenings, that she knew he was thinking of the past and what might have been.

He ran his tongue over the seam of her lips and pulled her tightly against him as she wrapped her arms around his neck. She'd missed him, too, he thought. Yes, she had. He lifted his head and looked at her eyes, half-closed, at her lips, rosy and wet, and the gap between her teeth that drove him crazy with lust for some reason. "I missed you, Mrs. Gentry," he whispered.

"I missed you, too." She looked at him from under her lashes.

"And I did buy everything you told me to buy, even the winter coat and the silk stockings."

He kissed her ear and ran his tongue around the edge of it. "You ordered silk stockings? Embroidered chemises?"

"Oh, yes. Lace drawers and filmy night things, too."

He groaned, feeling himself get hard against her stomach. She laughed softly against his cheek. "Come," he said. "Let's find this lemonade."

"And I went to a literary soiree! I met all sorts of interesting people and Miss McKellar introduced me to everyone as a published author. It was exciting and terrifying," she said with a laugh after they'd seated themselves outside on the benches on the stone patio. "Mr. McKellar, her brother, is smitten with your mother, although Olivia said that you and Matt may not like to hear that."

"What is he like?"

"He's attentive to everyone. The first night I met him, he was at the house for dinner several evenings, and escorted us to the theatre, oh my, the theatre, it was wondrous, and to a garden party at the home of a friend of Miss McKellar's, and on other visits, too. I was so glad some of my clothes were ready in time, so I didn't have to make my greetings in rags," she said, her eyes shining. "But I was saying, the first night I met him, he sat down beside me and asked me all kinds of questions about my writing and my family. He is the kind of person who draws out confidences and makes you feel as if you are the only person in the room. He's very attentive to Eleanor without ever seeming cloying and she is her same steady, unperturbed self, other than . . ." she trailed off and blushed.

"Other than when?"

"When we were at the dressmaker's, Mrs. Finch, the owner, and Eleanor were listing all the different things that I would need, and I said my husband didn't want me to forget silk stockings and . . . filmy night things."

"Well," he said and chuckled. "What did Mother say?"

"She cleared her throat and her ears were a bit pink and she said something about me not having a complete trousseau. Mrs. Finch said that I'd need a 'full selection of bedroom attire.' I was mortified at the time but there wasn't anything to be done about it, so I said, yes, a full set. You should have seen Nettie's and Olivia's faces!"

"Your sister and mine were there, too?"

"Yes, and then they dragged me back to Mrs. Finch's early the next morning without Eleanor or Miss McKellar and both ordered bedroom attire for themselves. Nettie asked if they had anything with feathers, of all things! What would someone do with feathers in the bedroom?"

Adam found himself dreading seeing his mother or sister or Nettie but also imagining Emmaline stretched out on their bed while he ran a feather up her creamy white thigh. He smiled at her then and thought their intimate life would be fine and if that was all they ever had between them, he hoped it would be enough.

He smiled at her then in such a way as to make her think that he knew exactly what to do with a feather in the bedroom. "What was she like?"

He tilted his head. "What was who like?"

"Josephine. What was she like?"

"She's gone from my life, Emmaline. You are my future."

"You think about her still." She shrugged. "Not all the time but you still do. What was she like?"

Adam looked off into the trees at the back of the Paradise property, and she thought he was imagining Josephine's face. It hurt a little. Not that she had expectations to replace the love of his life but still, it hurt a little. She wondered if it would always be like that. Would a dead woman always be between them?

"She was sophisticated and dedicated to her charities and to intellectual pursuits. She hosted a literary salon with her brother once a month that drew the best and the brightest and the most interesting persons from Washington. She was tall and slender. She was not a classical beauty, but she was very handsome and attractive" He turned his head to look at her. "But she was not you, Emmaline."

She *harrumphed*. "Obviously. I'm not tall and slender, and I wasn't even sure what a literary salon was until last week and the only charity I boast is when I don't kill my youngest brother. She must have been something. Really something to catch your eye and devotion."

"I felt as if I'd been struck by lightning when I met her for the first time," he said quietly and then looked at her and shook his head. "I shouldn't be saying this to you. I'm sorry."

"There's no need to be sorry. You wouldn't have said it if it wasn't true and I think, I really think, you and I are going to have to be truthful with each other if we're going to be happy, or at least, not unhappy for the next few decades. I've been hiding behind bluster for a lot of years and look where it got me. Expecting a child and not married to the father, whom I'd just met before letting him, well, you know. God, I'm mortified to think about that night and what a posturing ass I was, pretending to be sophisticated and knowledgeable and able to handle a few kisses and touches."

She turned her head to face him. "When did you get so wise?" he asked. "But I think you're right. I think we're going to have to be honest with each other. And I'm being honest when I tell you that I don't think of Josephine all that often. In fact, I don't think about her much at all and sometimes I feel guilty because of it, which is ridiculous! Josephine is no longer here to set an expectation so there isn't cause for guilt. Sometimes, though, an odd word or a picture or just the way the sun is shining on window glass sets me to think of a moment with her. I loved her when she was here on this earth and I think fondly of her in memory. I think of Aunt Bridget, too, having lost her not long before

Josephine. She lived with us from the time she sold her shop in town until her death and I spent plenty of afternoons helping her there when I was a young boy. She was irreverent and smart, and I loved her like a second mother but didn't realize it until she was gone."

"Grief has some lasting effects on us, I think," she said. "Jim felt responsible for us all when Daddy died, and the loss made me a little desperate. Jane won't argue with anyone and she told Betsy it's because she's terrified they will be dead in the next moment."

He stared at her then, letting his eyes wander over her face, making her feel as if he was memorizing the look of her. "I'll admit I'm a bit terrified, too, and maybe it has something to do with grief. I'm dreading the time you'll be gone to Philadelphia. I'm not sure how it happened, it seemed to come on gradually, but I don't quite remember the time before you were in my life."

She smiled ruefully and thought the same thing. What was life like before Adam Gentry? "So, not like a lightning strike."

He shook his head slowly and moved closer to her, staring at her lips, just inches from his own. "No," he whispered. "More like the surge of the ocean coming in slowly and then crashing into the shore, again and again, for eternity."

Ah, how sweet words could be, she thought, listening to the quickened patter of her heart and the soft breaths he took. "You should write books, Adam," she whispered. "You'll make the heroine fall in love with you."

"One author between us is enough, don't you think?" He grinned crookedly and kissed her.

"Jenny is probably watching us out the kitchen window," she said when they broke apart. "And I should finish the chapter I'm writing."

"I should check on the foals."

They both stood, and he clasped her hand as they walked toward the door of the house. She reached up and kissed his cheek. "I'll see you for dinner."

. . .

ADAM DIDN'T COME IN FROM THE STABLES UNTIL LATE afternoon. It was a blazing hot day even for mid-July. He wondered what had come over him to speak to Emmaline as he had earlier. What was it about her that made him confess rather than listen to others' confessions? He stopped at the water pump at the back of the house and stuck his face under it and rinsed his hands, shaking his head like a dog. He found his wife in the kitchens, her nose buried in a wicker basket, wearing one of her old skirts and a stained blouse.

"It is blasted hot out there," he said. "I've told everyone to take the day tomorrow and do as little as possible. The foals are down, and we could do with some relaxation."

She looked up at him and smiled. "Exactly what I thought! I've told Jenny, Mabel, and Beatrice to take the evening off. They've gone into Winchester in the wagon. They packed us a basket before they left. Let's go to the creek near Matthew's house where he's dammed it and swim."

Her eyes were shining, and she was smiling her gap-toothed smile. Her hair was mostly up but pieces were hanging down and clinging to her neck. He could see her fingers on her right hand were stained with ink, and maybe a spot or two on her cheek. She was lovely. How could he have ever wondered if he would be able to want her or complete the sex act with her without thinking of another woman. He wanted her all the time, and especially like this, excited and carefree.

"Swimming, Emmaline? Is that dignified enough for two old folks like us?"

She snorted. "Old? Speak for yourself and carry the basket. It weighs a ton."

He followed her out the back door, carrying the basket as he'd been told, and laughing. He was feeling lighthearted, which he hadn't been in a long while, and it felt good to take some time to drop the worries and concerns of business and family. She followed a trail through the woods, eventually meeting the path behind Matthew and Annie's house. He dropped the basket in the shade of the massive tree beside the creek and sat down to pull off his boots.

Emmaline unbuttoned her blouse and skirt and let them fall to the ground. She wasn't wearing a corset or petticoats or a bustle, just a chemise and her drawers.

"Annie told me that Matt is out of town overnight at the lumber mill," she said.

"He told me he was going to finalize the purchase papers. He should be back tomorrow."

"That's what Annie said."

"You stopped to see Annie?"

"Yes. She'll be staying in with the children tonight." She pulled her chemise over her head and untied her drawers, letting them fall to the ground. "There's soap and towels in the basket."

Emmaline turned and walked into the water, moaning at the coolness of it as she did. She had full breasts, a small waist, and rounded hips, and he was paralyzed watching her as her body sank below the water line, until she dove under, her white bottom popping up for a moment.

He stood slowly and walked to the edge of the creek in his stockinged feet, watching her swim in the dammed water. He did not feel as if he could move a muscle, that he might shatter into a thousand tiny pieces if he tried to. It was if he'd had landed in the midst of the most realistic erotic dream possible. But she wasn't a dream. She stopped swimming and looked back at him, crouched down in the water up to her shoulders.

"Would you bring me the soap? I want to wash my hair."

Adam squeaked out an embarrassing high-pitched yes. Perhaps the sound of his voice, as if he were thirteen years old and peeping through a window at a naked woman, was finally the thing that made him move. He pulled his shirt and undershirt over his head, yanked at his belt and pants buttons, and peeled off everything, including his drawers. He stood on one foot to pull off his sock, and then the other, all the while not taking his eyes from her.

"It seems to think I was staring at it," she said as she glanced at his midsection and smiled. "Don't forget the soap."

He turned to the picnic basket and dug through until he found the soap, feeling a bit ridiculous having an erection, completely naked, bent over a basket, not one hundred feet from his brother's house, even if brush and low trees blocked its sight. Emmaline had turned away from him, moving slowly with the current and humming, he could hear. He ran at the water, jumping at the last minute, feeling as foolish and childish as he did free and happy.

The water washed over her head when he hit. She quickly threw her wet hair back and slammed her hands down in front of him, splashing him in the face. He chased her across the creek as she shrieked and ran as fast as the water would allow. They were both laughing when he caught her.

"Here! Here's your soap!" he said as he pushed her under the water. She swam behind him and buckled his knees.

"Don't drop it!" she shouted and laughed after coming out of the water.

He wrapped his arms around her from behind, bringing her wet slick back against his bare chest and holding her there, her breasts resting on his forearm. They were both breathing hard as their laughter faded, moving against each other in rhythm. My God, he thought to himself, I'm falling in love with her. But that was impossible. He moved the wet ribbon of hair from the back of her neck and kissed her there. She turned in his arms, putting her hands on his shoulders, and looked up.

"This was a good idea on such a hot day, was it not?" she whispered.

He followed a drop of water with his finger from where it

dropped off of her chin to land on her breastbone. He watched it snake slowly between her breasts and then returned his gaze to her face, just inches from his. "Yes," he whispered back, dropping to his knees and bringing her to his side to laze about in the cool, moving water. "This was a perfect idea."

They floated together, and he closed his eyes, reveling in the feel of her, the weight of her body, alive and warm against his, feeling the sun flicker through the overhanging branches, still hot even as it began to set over the woods.

"Tell me about the story you're writing," he asked.

"Hmm. It's about a young woman who rescues a horse from being mistreated. She has to hide herself and the horse and stay ahead of the animal's owner. I suppose I'd call it an action adventure."

"Something like our marriage?" He grinned. "Without the horse, of course."

"Our marriage was more like a tragedy. With my miscarriage and your grief."

Her voice was somber, and he felt it, too. And it was a tragedy. "We were both numb, I think. I was drunk for months on end, and you were . . ."

"Terrified. Embarrassed. Sick. Humiliated. Even now, the memory of telling my mother, the look on her face, it turns my stomach and makes my hands shake."

"It seems like a long, long time ago in some ways," he said and turned his face to kiss her hair.

"I know. It seems forever ago. I still grieve for the baby I lost but it no longer colors my view of the future. For a while, it felt as though everything in my life would be wrong, would go wrong, and I would be alone in my struggles until someone buried me and that I would never reach the goals I'd set for myself. It doesn't feel like that any longer."

She'd described his deepest thoughts as well, that he would never feel a profound commitment or connection to another person, other than his family, and even then, he knew that the love he felt for his mother and siblings, and even their spouses, was not the same as the relationship he'd had with Josephine. But there was some burgeoning intimacy between him and his bride that was mostly due to very pleasing sexual relations. But not completely. There was some satisfaction knowing that she'd thought about leaving him, but hadn't. He'd thought about living his life out with her with distant courtesy and duty, but that wasn't the current reality, either.

"I'm shriveling up," she said as she turned out of his arms. She dipped her head back in the water and rubbed the soap she still held on her head. He took the sliver from her and washed his body and hair and they trudged out of the creek together.

He pulled on his short drawers after toweling off and sat down on the blanket she'd spread out. She put on her underclothes and sat down beside him to rub her hair dry with a towel and comb it. He lay back on the blanket, completely relaxed, restful, and calm. He wasn't worrying about anything more than what was packed to eat in the basket he'd carried. She turned to him, leaning back on her arms, her lips parted as she stared at his mouth. She leaned over him, her hair a curtain around their faces, and kissed him. There was no urgency, just a slow exploration with tongues and teeth and lips. He didn't want it to end, the privacy, the sense of isolation from daily living, the comfort of outdoor sounds and a light breeze. He reached his hand through her damp hair and held her closer.

* * *

EMMALINE SPENT A LITTLE MORE TIME THAN USUAL ON HER hair, which was never much, and wore a new pale green dress that had just arrived from Mrs. Finch's in Washington. Adam dressed in a dark suit with a tan shirt and a red tie and looked as handsome as it was possible for a man to look, she thought. They rode together in the gig for the short distance to the church in town, making her think of the last time she'd been there—her wedding day. Her mother had scolded her for not attending Sunday mornings now that she was feeling better and maybe she would again.

They sat in the second row beside Nettie and John, the children, and Olivia and behind her mother and Phillip. Jim was at the altar giving Betsy's hand to a smiling and red-faced Edwin. Jane stood beside Betsy as a bridesmaid, and Edwin's brother was beside him as best man.

Growing up, church had been every bit as social as a dance on Saturday night, and she was sometimes the subject of that gossip and some looks as well. She didn't think she could take any sly looks about her wedding and speculation about the loss of her child if she stood at the altar beside her sister. She'd had a long talk with Betsy and told her that she just wasn't ready to stand up in front of all the church folk and that she was sorry that her foolishness had led to that decision. Betsy had hugged her and kissed her and told her that she mustn't worry a bit about it. She apologized to Emmaline for staying away from her and for being angry and Emmaline has assured her she was forgiven, if there was anything at all to forgive. They'd had a long and rather vivid discussion of what Betsy might expect on her wedding night. She and Edwin were traveling to Middletown to stay over a few days at the hotel there for their honeymoon.

She tilted her head toward Adam and whispered, "I spoke to Betsy about her wedding night."

"Good God. I'm not sure if I want to know what you said."

"She does look beautiful, doesn't she?"

Adam nodded. "She looks lovely. Her groom looks as though he's being strangled."

"I think he adores Betsy."

"It looks like it."

She pulled herself close to his ear and whispered, "He'll adore her more by tomorrow morning."

He looked at her, his eyes darkened, as he started to grin. "Mrs. Gentry. You wicked girl. You will have to tell me in detail what you told your sister."

Nettie's daughter Rachel leaned over to them. "You mustn't talk in church. Daddy will be mad."

CHAPTER 12

Emmaline looked out the train window as it slowed coming into the Thirty-Second Street Station in Philadelphia. Adam was beside her, having insisted that he accompany her and get her settled at Clair House. He wanted a "lay of the land" he'd said when she'd told him he needn't come with her. It would have been a burden worrying about her luggage and trunk and getting to Clair House but she was certain she could have managed; she'd *wanted* to manage on her own for the first time. But he wouldn't hear of it. And they'd argued.

She was still a bit angry, truth be known, but she thought she understood why he was so adamant. He was concerned, which was not a strong enough word, for her safety, imagining all sorts of troubles that could befall a young woman on her own. His distress was endearing in some ways and aggravating in others.

"Here we are," he said as the train slowed to a stop.

She stood in front of him, waiting to disembark, excited and nervous beyond anything she'd ever dreamed. She was dancing from foot to foot, licking her lips, and wringing her hands at her waist. She was here. She was finally here!

Adam went ahead of her down the steps onto the platform, to

turn back and reach for her hand. She looked out at the station, at the mass of people going this way and that, wondering where they would find her luggage. She took his hand and stepped down, glad then she had his hand to hold as she could no longer see over the hats on the women and past the tall men, to see where she should go next.

"We're going to head for the doors straight ahead!" he shouted over the roar of the crowd as he pointed. She nodded and followed close behind, keeping her little drawstring bag tight against her waist. The crowd thinned as they moved away from the train, now loading passengers. Adam held her hand as he maneuvered around their fellow travelers to a ticket agent.

He found where they were to get her trunks and bags and went about securing them a carriage to take them to Clair House. He'd made reservations for himself at a small hotel near the school. Soon they were on their way in the open-top conveyance and she was glad the breeze was cooling her heated cheeks. Adam found her hand and held it tightly.

They arrived within a few minutes at a large brick home on a busy tree-lined street, between other large homes. They'd just passed Adam's hotel, a few blocks before arriving, near other shops, a printer's, and a bank with iron grates over the windows. The door of Clair House was opened by an older Negro woman wearing a black skirt and a stiffly starched white blouse covered by a gray apron.

"May I help you?"

Emmaline cleared her throat several times and felt Adam's hand close around her elbow. "Yes. Yes, you may. Is this Clair House? I am to be enrolled here, I think."

Just then a tall, thin, bespectacled man appeared behind the woman. "Miss Somerset, I presume," he said. "We've been expecting you. I'm Mr. Clair. This is Mrs. Mingo, our housekeeper. Do come in. I'll send Herbert out for your luggage."

"It's Mrs. Gentry," Adam said from behind her. "We're recently married. I'm Adam Gentry."

They were escorted into a large, bright parlor, every shelf, table space, and mantle inch filled with figurines and pictures, with comfortable-looking couches and chairs in several seating groups. Adolphus Clair shook Adam's hand and offered him whiskey instead of the coffee being prepared at that moment, which he declined. He sat down beside her while their host went in search of his wife. Emmaline's stomach fluttered, and she felt as if she couldn't get enough breath. She'd read about Clair House in a newspaper article when she was only ten or eleven years old. The thought of attending had consumed her for years, and now having arrived, she would admit, she was overwhelmed.

"I never really believed I would ever get here," she whispered.

"You are here, Emmaline. You deserve to be here," he said and looked around the room. "Seems to be a very cozy and well-maintained house, does it not?"

"Does it? I haven't noticed."

He squeezed her hand. "Breathe. Easy in, easy out."

The door opened, and a short, stout middle-aged woman came rushing in, ribbons flying, with a broad smile on her plump face. "Miss Somerset! I hear you have been struck by Cupid's arrow and are now Mrs. Gentry! How wonderful! I was likewise assailed by love when my Adolphus came courting. He was so romantic, so enamored of me, and me of him! And we are still of one mind, as the poets say." She leaned down, hugged Emmaline, and then turned her head toward her husband. "Just look at him. No finer specimen of manhood walks this earth."

Adolphus Clair stood tall and still, and apparently unperturbed at his wife's ramblings. His hair was combed over a bald spot on the top of his head and his glasses sat crookedly on his nose. His gray suit was finely made and fit his rail-thin six-foot frame well. "Mrs. Mingo has brought the tray, dear. Will you pour?" he said.

"Oh, yes," she said and fluttered away as the cart was wheeled into the room. "Oh, yes, my love. I've forgotten myself, yet again."

Emmaline and Adam accepted the coffee and waited until Mrs. Clair settled into the chair across from them, her husband seating himself in the chair beside her.

"Now," Mrs. Clair began, leaning forward in her seat. "Tell us about your writing. Tell us what you write. Tell us what you are working on now."

"I have just begun a new novel. I don't have a title, but it is about a young woman who steals away a horse that is being mistreated by its owner and their adventures hiding and evading a sheriff. I've just recently had another story accepted by Beadle's."

"By Beadle's?" Mr. Clair asked, nodding and smiling. "Well done. I am always glad to see young writers make a living at their craft."

Emmaline shrugged. "I hardly make a living, sir. I lived with my family until I was married and of course, now live with my husband. He's very successful, which makes me very fortunate."

Mrs. Clair laughed, and Adam smiled at the woman she saw when she turned to look at him.,

"Let me explain our regular schedule, Mrs. Gentry," Mrs. Clair said. "We do classes every morning from eight until luncheon. The afternoon is for completing your assignments and if there is time still available, then you may work at whatever personal project you wish. In the evening, we sometimes gather here or in the garden, if the weather cooperates, to talk about our work or just relax and regain our energy. We do attend some literary gatherings together, and you are welcome to join us. We also are often guests of some good families in the city who admire our work here at Clair House or are supporters of the arts. Sundays are a free day, and there are churches within walking distance."

Adam cleared his throat. "I thought I'd open an account for my wife at the bank we passed by on the way here, near some shops."

"The Bigelow Bank?" Mr. Clair asked, and Adam nodded. "Good choice. Within walking distance for Mrs. Gentry to withdraw funds if need be, although all her meals and board are provided with the tuition. I have received your check and Mrs. Gentry is paid in full."

Adam glanced at her before turning back to Mr. Clair. "Will there be someone to accompany my wife when she goes on errands and such?"

"Adam. I will be fine. I have managed to take care of myself up until now and I think I will be able to continue," she said, feeling her face turn hot with a blush.

"It will be different than Winchester, as we have discussed," he said quietly and turned back to Mr. Clair. "Will there be someone to accompany her when she goes out? I would like to be certain that she'll be chaperoned."

"The women almost always go together whenever there is an errand to be run or just for exercise, and Mrs. Mingo's son is the all-about boy here and can escort your wife if need be. He is eighteen years old and is a big, strong young man. Our students' safety and comfort are very important to us," he said.

Mrs. Clair leaned forward and patted Emmaline's knee. "You will make friends quickly, my dear. I'm sure you will find a young woman who becomes a particular friend and then you can do your errands and such together. Let us go see your rooms now and put your husband's mind at ease about your stay with us."

Emmaline's heart was pounding and her jaw was so tight she could feel her teeth grinding together. *How dare he!* She couldn't recall ever being so furious and so embarrassed. She stepped away from his hand as he reached out to take her arm, so angry she wasn't even able to concentrate on Mrs. Clair's instructions about laundry and schedules for the shared bathing room.

Once in her rooms, however, the fury subsided. Mrs. Clair hurried her into the sleeping room, which held a small bed with a brass headboard covered with a bright quilt opposite a finely carved bureau with a large framed mirror above it. There was a rocker beside a narrow window with chintz curtains pulled back to one side, its sill wide enough to hold a framed picture or a book.

They walked back into her sitting area where Mr. Clair and Adam stood, a cozy room with a double window looking out onto the gardens at the back of the house and shaded by a large tree. But her eyes couldn't leave the one item that stood under that window. A desk. A large desk with drawers on either side of the leg hole with a polished top holding a felt pad and books standing against heavy metal bookends shaped like horse heads. It was her desk. It would be where she would learn and stretch her mind, and maybe grow as a writer . . . and as a person.

She walked slowly to the desk, past Mrs. Clair, no longer aware of others in the room, running her hand over the back of a wooden chair that was fit with wheels on its legs. She moved the chair around, hearing the smooth glide of the rollers against the waxed hardwood floor. She touched the books, a dictionary, a thesaurus, and a book of riddles, the sun glinting in the window, shining on the desktop other than where the felt pad lay. The space, the view, the furniture itself was everything she'd dreamed of. She swallowed loudly and closed her eyes, hating the intensity of the emotions she was feeling, as if she stood on a precipice looking at her dream within her reach. There was only one person she wished to share the wonder of it all with and he stood behind her, she could feel his eyes on her. She turned to face him, trying desperately to refrain from running into his embrace. He was staring back at her, his dark eyes boring into hers, maybe waiting for her to come to him, she didn't know. She took one deep breath and broke the gaze, turning to Mrs. Clair.

"This is—" she began, stopping to clear her throat and gather herself, "this is exactly as I'd always pictured a real writer's retreat whenever I imagined what it would be like to indulge myself and write every day."

Mrs. Clair rushed to her and clasped her hands. "Oh, my dear. I am so glad. You may be inspired here. Many are."

ADAM CLEARED HIS THROAT. "MR. CLAIR? CAN YOU recommend a good restaurant nearby? I'm staying one night and catching the morning train, but I thought I'd take my wife out to dinner before I go."

"There is no need, Adam," Emmaline said. "And I would like to begin the routine here as soon as possible. Now, in fact."

He would have liked her to tell him what she'd been thinking when she looked at the desk under the window. She'd stood for several minutes staring at it and he'd seen her shoulders rise and fall with deep breaths. She'd looked at him, connected to him somehow, and then quickly begun a conversation with Mrs. Clair. He knew she was angry. He'd embarrassed her, but he wanted to make it perfectly clear that her safety was his concern, and he fully intended to fulfill his duty to her regardless of how she felt about it. He supposed he could have waited and spoken to Mr. Clair privately, but it was too late for that now. He was hoping a dinner out together would make them part on agreeable terms, but she'd punished him instead.

They walked down the wide staircase together and he turned to her. "Emmaline, I want to take you with me to the bank and see to transferring funds and making you acquainted with the manager there."

"That is wise, Mr. Gentry," Mr. Clair said.

He thought for a moment that she would refuse—and he really didn't know what he would do or say if she did—but she seemed to think better of it.

"Let me get my bag. I left it in the parlor."

Mrs. Clair smiled up at him. "Now don't you worry about her. Not one minute. We take very good care of our ladies, both their safety and comfort and reputation. Your wife will be perfectly fine here."

"I'm sure you're right," he said. "And thank you for your diligence. Mrs. Gentry is precious to me."

"Of course, she is," Mrs. Clair said. "Anyone can see that you two are a love match!"

He smiled at the woman, not willing to publicly disabuse her of her romantic ideals, especially as the thin thread he and Emmaline had been forming was stretching. He didn't want to leave her angry. She went directly to the door after she'd retrieved her bag, waiting without a glance at him.

He escorted her out the door, down the walkway, and turned onto a graveled path under massive oak trees toward the commerce area. He winged his arm for her to take and she looked at him as if he was the lowliest worm she'd ever stepped on. He couldn't stop himself from chuckling even knowing he was risking his peace if he did. She turned sharply.

"I don't find anything humorous about you humiliating me."

"I had no plans to humiliate you." He hurried to keep up with her pace. "Slow down. There's no need to run."

She reduced her speed, her eyes concentrated ahead, her lips pursed. "No, there is not."

They arrived at the bank and were introduced to the manager there. Adam had a check with him and made it out to the bank, handing it over to the manager, who stood to process it. "There is five hundred dollars in the account. If you need more, let me know. I'm sure we'll be corresponding regularly."

The look she gave him made him wonder if they would be corresponding at all. He was pleased to see that the manager took Emmaline to introduce her to the two tellers assisting customers. The manager reviewed the bank's security procedures and asked if Adam would like to view the vault.

"No, but thank you," he said and turned to Emmaline. "Do you have any questions for Mr. McCollough?"

"I don't. Thank you for your time," she said.

They left the bank, and he saw a park ahead across the street. He guided her between carriages and past excited children with their nurses. They took a path bearing toward the general direction of Clair House and he found a bench in a secluded area. She sat, realizing, he hoped, that they needed to speak privately. He sat beside her.

"I'm sorry," he said finally, eliciting a glance from her. "I should have spoken to Mr. Clair privately. I didn't mean to humiliate you."

"I am not a child and I did feel humiliated. You talked as if I was not sitting next to you."

"No, you are not a child but I'm guessing you've not been to a large city all that often or if ever, other than when you recently went to Washington with our sisters." He looked at her. She arched a brow and he was certain he was right. "Living here won't be like Winchester. Any stranger there is identified immediately as just that. A stranger. Everyone in town would know that your brother or myself would not allow anyone to bother you. Let alone the fact that everyone from Mr. Winston at the Mercantile to Jasper at the stables would never allow a stranger to approach you. It won't be like that here. There are some who may have evil intentions all over a city."

"You act as though there are not plenty of fine respectable people here," she said.

"Of course, there are. Mr. and Mrs. Clair seem to be well aware of their responsibilities and they seem to take them seriously. I'm glad of that. But there are seven other women, from what I understand, who will be here at the same time as you and they will have to attend all of you. I cannot help it if I need to be assured of *your* safety."

She stood then and turned to him, red in the face. "I am aware that I must be careful. I'm not frivolous. I've been waiting all my life it seems for this opportunity and you made me feel as if I was just a silly girl unable to recognize that there may be dangers that I am unaccustomed to facing. We have spoken of this several times, even this morning on the train ride here, and I have assured you every time that I would be on my guard and cautious," she said, her voice rising. "You just don't seem to believe me."

He'd stood when she had, and he glared at her now, as she made her accusations. "I believe you! Of course, I believe you. I just don't think you are as aware as you should be. I'm concerned about you!"

"Aware? What do you mean aware? What am I not *aware* of, Adam Gentry!"

"You are not always aware of people's intent. They can hurt you and will and I won't be here to stop them!"

"You act as though I go through my life not paying the least attention to what is going on around me!" she shouted.

"You didn't know what was going on the night you . . . you were led astray."

He was devasted then, watching her face crumble, her shoulders drop, her hand slowly come up to cover her mouth. Her eyes went to the ground and she seated herself as if she'd been pushed onto the bench. He could see her lip trembling and watched as a tear dropped onto her folded hands.

"Emmaline, dear," he said softly. "I should have never brought that up. That was wrong of me."

"You don't trust me," she whispered and gulped a swallow.

"That is not true."

"I would never be free with another man. I'm married."

"Of course, you wouldn't. That's not what I meant."

"I think that is exactly what you meant. Take me to Clair House, please."

"I don't want to leave us like this," he said and reached for her hand. She snatched it away and held the strings of her purse.

She stood and walked away from him and he followed until

they came to a gated path directly across from Clair House. She turned to him then, focusing on his four-in-hand tie and not his eyes.

"I will be perfectly fine the rest of the way. You may stay and watch me until I am inside," she said and looked in his eyes. "Thank you for everything. For the tuition. For getting me here. I think it's best if you went on your way to your hotel now. Have a safe trip tomorrow."

She unlatched the gate and went through, watching until there was no carriage coming and walking across the street, up the narrow walk, and in through the front door, never turning once to look at him. He ran a hand through his hair and thought about what an ass he'd been. He supposed he should consider himself lucky that she hadn't punched him in the nose or walloped him with her purse.

CHAPTER 13

Emmaline slept little that night and had nearly convinced herself it was because she was in a new bed, in a strange city, and she was excited and nervous to finally be at Clair House. But the truth of the matter, she finally accepted, was that her argument with Adam played over and again in her mind. She couldn't stop a flush from going up her face when she recalled Adam asking Mr. Clair a *second* time whether she would be accompanied when she went out and even went so far as to use the word *chaperoned*. As if she were a fifteen-year-old girl or the type to be free with another man.

Once or twice, she'd started to think that what Adam had said didn't sound as bad to others as it had to her, but she was determined to be angry. This was not a small transgression in her mind. Or she wouldn't let it be, in any case. She knew she was being petty. She couldn't help herself. She was hurt, and hurt deeply, and she'd rarely had the experience of being wounded emotionally, as she avoided most people and cared little for others' opinions. Apparently, she cared very much for her husband's.

Emmaline rose as the sun came up and rubbed her eyes, gritty from little sleep. She washed and put on a new tan twill skirt and shirt, lightweight for the warm end-of-summer weather. She placed her new manuscript on the desk with her fountain pens. She turned to a knock on the door, thinking Mrs. Clair was coming to check on her. She opened the door and found a young woman, probably her age, standing in the hall.

"Good morning," the woman said in a high-pitched and thready voice. "My name is Violet Dunderson. I was wondering if you'd like me to show you to the dining room since this is your first morning."

"Thank you, Violet. That would be very nice. My name is Emmaline Somerset, or rather, Emmaline Gentry. I'm recently married."

Violet tilted her head to the side and held her clasped hands to her chest. "To that imposing handsome fellow that you were with yesterday?"

"Adam Gentry. Yes. That is my husband. We married in the spring."

"How lovely!" Violet reached her hand out to link Emmaline's arm. "We're going to have a very, very busy day today, Emmaline, may I call you Emmaline, or would you prefer Mrs. Gentry?"

"Emmaline is fine."

She pulled her door shut and followed a fluttering Violet down the hallway to the top of the stairs. She took a deep breath and thought that her dreams had finally arrived.

At six o'clock in the evening Emmaline trudged into her rooms and toed off her shoes. She was mentally and physically exhausted but thankfully hadn't had time to stew about her husband. The morning classes were a challenge to her and she recognized that she would have to study and work harder than the rest of the students, who'd all graduated from college or been enrolled in advanced English classes. None were married, or, as in her case, had been expecting a child out of wedlock. One young lady was only seventeen years old. Emmaline felt ancient and . . . not virtuous, even knowing that that was ridiculous.

"Emmaline?" she heard Violet say. "May I come in?"

She didn't really want to talk to anyone at that moment, but Violet had been a dear to her all day. When she opened the door, Violet handed her an envelope. It said *Emmaline Gentry* in Adam's bold script. She looked at it for a few long moments, rubbing her thumb over the dried ink he'd written and thinking about how angry and hurt she'd been at this time yesterday. She laid the envelope on the desk and turned to Violet.

"He delivered it early this morning and Mrs. Clair laid it on her desk to give to you and forgot all about it."

"Won't you come in for a moment? Or are you heading down to the garden with the others?"

"I am not," Violet said. "I'm a trifle tired."

"Perhaps I could get us a glass of iced tea from the kitchen and we could sit here and get to know each other," Emmaline said. "I've opened the window and there's a nice breeze."

"Oh." Violet clapped her hands together softly, looking at Emmaline wistfully. "That would be wonderful. I'll just step into my room for a moment and freshen myself."

Emmaline had already made herself known to the Clair House cook, Miss Gertrude Flanders, a tiny woman, happily humming and overseeing the cleanup of the evening meal. Soon Emmaline was climbing the stairs with a tray carrying a pitcher of tea, two glasses filled with chipped ice, and a plate of lemon cookies. It made her think of Paradise and Mabel.

Emmaline left her room door open and Violet joined her, still wearing the frilly high-necked dress she'd worn all day. Emmaline had changed into an old skirt and shirt that she left open at the collar. She plopped down at her desk chair and Violet sat down in the only other chair in the room.

"I can come back another evening, if you'd prefer to read your letter." Violet nodded to the envelope still lying on Emmaline's desk unopened.

Emmaline shook her head. "No. I'll read it later. Please tell me about yourself. How did you come to Clair House?"

Violet blushed. "It has always been a dream of mine. I've been writing since I was young girl and as much as I love it here, I feel terribly guilty. You see, my parents are elderly, having had me late in life, and my father is ten years older than my mother. He is bedridden now, and she is of a sickly constitution." She sniffed, touching a lace- edged hanky to her nose. "Of course, they are well cared for while I am here. I would have never done it if my father hadn't insisted. I am quite satisfied to care for them rather than pursue my writing, but Father wouldn't hear of it."

"Are you able to get away to visit them?"

"Oh, yes. I go almost every Sunday after church and some Saturday evenings, too. Father sends his carriage for me and I visit with them both. Where are you from, Emmaline? When will you get to see your husband next?"

"Six months from now, I think, unless I travel to Winchester for the Christmas holiday."

"Six months! But won't you miss him dreadfully?"

Emmaline stared at the envelope. She would miss him. She already did, even as angry as she was. Was that the nature of marriages? That she could be furious with him and still wonder what he was doing and if he was thinking of her. Or was it possible that Nettie was right—that she was not immune to soft feelings and that she had fallen in love with her husband. And knowing that he didn't trust her, that he wasn't convinced she was aware enough to understand the dangers the city presented, that perhaps he thought she would have relations with another man, hung on her.

"I already miss him."

Violet patted her hand. "Of course, you do. He's so very hand-some and gentleman-like."

"Yes. Yes, he is," she replied. Violet said good night shortly after, and Emmaline wondered if it was because she'd stared at the envelope, turning it over and again in her hand and saying little. She washed her face and hands, pulled on her favorite nightgown, and climbed into bed to read.

Dear Emmaline,

I did not feel right leaving Philadelphia without at least speaking to you further on the subject we argued on yesterday afternoon. If you remember when I proposed marriage to you, you asked me how I could respect you. I told you then, and I'll repeat it here, whatever happened that night, was just a small part of a life you have lived well. I've never, ever thought that you found yourself in that situation because you were without discretion or character. I thought you were taken advantage of and I still believe that after coming to know you. I should have never said what I did, and I am sorry. I would never, ever suspect you of having some sort of relationship with another man. I trust you implicitly, Emmaline, even when I am frustrated.

But that does not diminish my concern. I find your writing explains much about your person. You're creative and sometimes everyday realities escape your notice as you are thinking on a higher plane than us mere mortals. I think it explains why you couldn't be bothered with a wardrobe and why the intricacies of managing a household such as Paradise seem overwhelming to you, although I believe you could do it and do it well if you wanted.

While I would never deny you this opportunity, although I don't think I could stop you if I tried, it has caused me hours of concern. My duty as a husband is to see to your safety and comfort and it is difficult for me to have you so far away. I know you will be careful, and that Mr. and Mrs. Clair are responsible people.

My dearest wish is that you are happy, having reached a goal you set for yourself as a young girl. I'm exceptionally proud of you and find myself bragging to others about my wife, 'the writer,' as if I have something to do with your abilities.

Sincerely and with respect,

Adam

SHE READ AND REREAD THE LETTER UNTIL THE HOUSE WAS quiet and settled. Was it possible he was right? Was it possible that she was a bit scatterbrained? Especially when she was concentrating on writing a story? She remembered Betsy complaining to her that she didn't pay any attention when she was telling her something, even if it was important, like the first time Edwin had said he would talk to Jim about courting her. Betsy had thrown something at her head that day, knocking her fountain pen to the floor, leaving a trail of ink down her skirts. Betsy had left the room in a huff and called for Jane.

It was true, probably. She'd never wanted to go to the seamstresses for new things, mostly because it would have interrupted the little time she'd had for her writing. Other things just never seemed that important. She'd done her chores, worked at the mercantile, and sequestered herself in her room at the small desk there, barely big enough to turn her pages without knocking a stack onto the floor, and kept to herself.

Were her and Adam's reactions to all of this just a case of her nerves, his concerns, and a misunderstanding? He did apologize for saying what he did to Mr. Clair, and just thinking about it made her angry. But was she justified? She thought perhaps she was and she thought he knew very well that he'd embarrassed her and while not regretful of his concerns, he was apologetic for how he'd said it. He thought about things from a different perspective, that was certain. Was that the nature of men and women? She knew that what was significant to her brother Jim, or even Phillip, was often very different from what her mother and her sisters thought. Had she not seriously considered that her husband, a man, would also view the world through a different lens? Good Lord, was she this scatterbrained?

Had she not considered that she was now *married*? For good

and forever tied to this one person and that there would be ups and downs and, undoubtedly, some unhappiness. That there would be a man who would surpass in importance all things and people that were previously important to her, even the precious ones like her nephew and niece. It was a good thing that she cared for Adam Gentry in the way that she did. He was her husband. They would argue and be angry and make up. She closed her eyes thinking of Adam kissing her when they were both naked and panting with need, impatient to join bodies, and be one. The bed felt very empty without him by her side. Emmaline longed for their easy teasing and trust in all things in their bedroom, and outside of it, that she'd become accustomed to.

* * *

"HAVE YOU HEARD FROM EMMALINE?" JIM ASKED ADAM AS THEY stood side by side helping Matt move a large rock behind his house that now was wrapped with iron chains.

"No," he said. "I have not. I've written every day, but I've not gotten a letter."

"Mother received one yesterday," Jim said while guiding the horses dragging the rock from its place.

"Hold up, Jim," Matt said. "We've got to get this chain wrapped differently, but let's take a break. Here comes Annie with something to drink."

Adam leaned on the shovel he was holding. Emmaline had sent her mother a letter and not responded to his? He was more annoyed than he could account for. He took the cold glass of water from Annie and kissed the top of little Teddy's head where he stood holding his mother's hand. Matt tickled his son, picked him up and tossed him into the air, eliciting giggles and screams.

"Put him down, Matthew," Annie said. "He's just eaten."

Adam turned to Jim, now sitting down on one of the logs they would use to roll the boulder. "Did you read the letter?" he asked, keeping his tone casual.

Jim shrugged. "Livie's meal didn't turn out so good so we went to my mother's last evening. She read it out loud three times. She hung on every word Emmaline had written, smiling and telling Jane and Phillip that their sister had worked very hard in school and had been rewarded and how proud she was of her."

Adam *harrumphed*.

"It's strange, though. Mother never fussed too much over Emmaline when we were growing up, probably because she was always independent. Now she can't stop talking about her. I think Mother's feeling a bit guilty. Emmaline is doing fine, though, sounds like."

Adam stared off into the woods, thinking of the letters he wrote every night and sent with the stable boy to Witherspoon to mail. It made him want to get on his horse and ride to Philadelphia and see her with his own eyes and shake her by the shoulders and ask her why she'd not written. And kiss her. Oh yes, he wanted to kiss her. He wanted to touch that gap between her teeth with his tongue. These past few weeks had been more than he could take. He missed her wit, her company, and her soft, warm body to curl around in bed. A tap on his arm nearly pushed him over.

"I'm talking to you," Matt said as Annie walked to the house. Teddy turned and waved as he held his mother's hand.

"He's thinking about his wife," Jim said.

Adam shook his head and sat down beside his brother-in-law. "No, I'm not. Well, yes, I am. We had an argument before I left Philadelphia. I write her every day, and haven't heard from her yet."

"What is it? Two months, now?" Jim asked.

"And you write her every day?" Matt said.

"I do."

"What was the argument about?" Matt asked. "Were you stupid?"

Adam nodded. "I think maybe."

They sat silently drinking their water waiting, Adam supposed, for him to elaborate. Maybe it would be good for him to unburden himself. Maybe these two young knuckleheads, although that was not a fair description, had some advice for him. They were married, after all. So, he told them.

"She was embarrassed by my comment to Clair, and then I brought up the night she . . . she got with . . ."

"You didn't," Matt said as he shook his head.

"Well, I was trying to impress on her that sometimes she doesn't pay attention to everything going on around her and that people can take advantage of a young woman like that. She thought I brought it up because I didn't trust her to . . ." Adam mumbled.

"Trust her to what?" Matt asked.

Adam cleared his throat. "Trust her to be faithful." He held up his hands to Jim in surrender. "I didn't mean that, I never thought that, but I wasn't very articulate, and she was yelling at me. Letting me have it with both barrels."

"What did she say then?" Jim asked.

"She didn't say much at first. Just plopped down on the park bench looking miserable, and saying she'd never be free with another man, that she was married. Then she dried her eyes, thanked me for bringing her to Clair House and for the tuition. She walked away to the door of the school and never looked back."

Every time he pictured her face and heard her words in that stiff, formal voice she'd used that afternoon, he got a little sick to his stomach, and wanted to stop thinking his own thoughts, which was impossible. He looked at Matt and Jim now staring at him. "I apologized. For both things. In person and in a letter."

"Had you talked to Emmaline about your worries before that day?"

"Yes, of course. I couldn't get it out of mind that she was going to be away from home and that something might happen. I talked to her about it several times, in fact."

"Several times?"

"Yes!" Adam said as he stood and began to pace. "Sometimes Emmaline is so caught up in her own thinking that she doesn't always realize what's going on around her. Anyone could snatch her bag on the way to the bank or even . . . I can't think about that. I wanted her to be wary."

"Adam," Matt said. "Sit down."

He sat down again beside Jim, and Matt crouched in front of him, putting him at eye level. Matt stared at him for several long seconds.

"She's not Josephine. She's not going to die just because she's not here."

Adam took a deep breath, feeling the anger wind up inside him, gritting his teeth, and making his fists curl. "This is nothing like that!" he shouted. "Nothing. I was in love with Josephine at the time."

"We know," Matt said. "Feel free to wallop me, or Jim, if you need to punch something or someone."

"I don't need to hit either of you idiots. I just need to make sure that my wife is safe. She's in a city she's not familiar with. She's as stubborn as any woman I've ever met."

"And you're in love with her," Jim said softly.

"Look, Jim. I'm sure you'd like to think that your sister and I have ended up falling in love, but it's just not true. I respect her and admire her. I'm happy to say we're married and I think she feels exactly the same way."

"You got it bad, brother," Matt said, shaking his head.

"Bullshit. I'm not in love with anyone. I like her. I respect her. But love, not doing that again."

"Like you have any control over it." Jim barked a laugh. "Sounds like me trying to talk myself out of it."

"You were really an ass, Somerset," Matt said and grinned at Jim. "I knew I loved Annie from early on, but I was just too much of a chickenshit coward to tell her."

"I'm not in love with Emmaline," Adam said.

"Okay, brother." Matt put his hands on his knees and pushed himself up to stand.

Adam followed. "Don't use that tone on me."

"What tone is that, Adam, lover of Emmaline?" he said.

Adam saw red and heard Jim laughing in the background. He let loose his right fist on his brother's chin and had some satisfaction as Matt's head snapped back. He followed with two short fast punches to Matt's middle. He stepped back waiting for him to respond, pulling his fists up to cover his chin, but Matt's arms hung loose at his sides.

"Come on. Come on! Hit me back!"

Matt shook his head and wiped blood from his chin. "Nope. I'm not mad at you or anybody else."

"You should be, damn it! Come on! Hit me!"

"Not going to do it. I do think you might have loosened a tooth, though," Matt said, smiling. "Hit Jim this time."

Adam looked at Jim, now standing beside Matt, his hands in his pockets. He rubbed his face and turned away from them both. What an ass he was! Here he was hitting his brother and nearly punching his sister's husband because he couldn't reconcile the thought that maybe, just maybe, he'd fallen in love with his wife. He turned without looking at either of them and started the walk home. *They can pull that damn rock out on their own.*

"HERE IS ANOTHER LETTER, EMMALINE!" VIOLET SAID FROM her doorway.

Emmaline turned in her chair. "Oh, thank you."

"Your husband is especially attentive! What a lucky wife you are."

"I suppose I am." She accepted the letter from her friend. "Except I'm not feeling very lucky. He has written me faithfully every day for two months, and I have not written him back once. Now I don't know what to say!"

"Are you still angry with him?"

Emmaline shook her head. "No. We're going to have disagreements and even though he said something that was hurtful, I don't think he intended to hurt me, and perhaps some of his observations are correct. This marriage business is confusing at first."

"Then write him! He must be most anxious to hear from you."

"I just don't know how to start."

"I know. We'll write a poem to him. An ode."

Emmaline smiled at the hopeful look on Violet's face. "A poem?"

"We'll be doing lessons in poetry very soon, so we'll consider this practice."

"We can start after dinner," Emmaline said. "Will you walk with me to the grocer and the bank before mealtime?"

"Of course! Let me get my cloak. It's cold out there."

Violet and Emmaline walked swiftly as there was a definite chill in the air and dark clouds that might bring rain hung overhead. Emmaline got the special coffee grounds she liked at the grocer and withdrew money at the bank as one of the students was leaving school and Mrs. Clair was organizing a group gift for her. Violet chattered on the way home, as they walked quickly, arms linked, toward Clair House.

At the warehouse building they passed a block from the bank, Emmaline could have sworn she saw someone scoot through the door just as they got close to it. But that was impossible. She'd never once seen a buggy or a person near the building and Mr. Clair said it was abandoned, although he was concerned that squatters would take up residence there. Maybe he was right. When they walked past the door, the hair on the back of Emmaline's neck stood up, sending a chill down her back. She looked quickly at the recessed doorway but saw nothing through the grimy round window. She gripped her umbrella tightly and hurried Violet along.

ADAM STOOD ON THE LANDING OF THE SECOND FLOOR OF Paradise as workmen pushed and pulled a massive desk up the staircase. Thank goodness Mother had installed a grand wide one during one of the many additions that were made to the house or they would have never gotten it to the second floor.

"Here, down here," he said and pointed, leading the workers toward Olivia's old bedroom. He'd had all the furniture removed to the attics and the walls painted a pale gray. The rug had been dragged outside and beaten and the floors polished. Jenny had hung new white draperies at the two long windows that over looked the back patios and woods. Adam stood there now as the desk was fitted between them, looking out at what he thought was one of the best views of the Paradise property. He was looking forward to surprising Emmaline.

The desk he'd had shipped from Washington with a matching wooden chair, along with an overstuffed dark red armchair that now sat beside the fireplace. A woodworker from Winchester had built bookshelves that covered the opposite wall from floor to ceiling. He hoped she would like it. He'd watched her that day at Clair House looking at the desk in her room, knowing that it had meant something to her. Symbolized something significant. He realized now that he'd been hurt that she'd not come to him that day.

He thanked the workmen and looked around the room. He'd decided not to add anything to the desk or mantel or bookshelves. He wanted Emmaline to make it her own in her own way.

He looked up from his musing when Jenny knocked at the open door. She was smiling broadly.

"Mr. Adam? A letter has come for you."

"A letter? You can put it on my desk, Jenny. Thank you."

"Oh." She looked at the envelope in her hand. "Please let us know how Mrs. Gentry is doing."

He walked to her. "From my mother, you say." He reached for the letter.

"No, Mr. Adam. From your wife."

He held it in his hand until he was sure Jenny had gone. He sat down on the red chair and pulled out the paper.

My dearest husband Adam
  So far away in Winchester,
  Wondering what has happened to his madam

She's writing pretty words of poetry
  And composing themes for novels
  Wondering if her husband will appreciate her coquetry

She's been a poor letter writer
  And he's been fine
  She'll have to say she's sorry to make her heart lighter.

Adam,
  As you can read above I will never find a magazine or publisher for my poetry as I attempt to apologize to you for not replying to all of your letters. At first, I was stewing in my own anger and then so much time had gone by that I just did not know how to begin. My friend Violet convinced me that poetry was just the thing, but she has given up on my verses after

two evenings of trying to help me. She said I was really spectacularly bad at it and I agree.

I miss you.

I work very hard during the week at classes and have to study most evenings as many of the women here have their college degree in English or literature. But I love it here. I love being able to write even when I'm not sure how to begin or end an assignment. I have also been working very hard on my next novel. Mrs. Clair was right. This place can be inspirational.

I miss you.

I promise to write more often. Please tell my family and all of yours that I'm doing well and learning as much as I can while I have this wonderful opportunity. Tell Mabel that the cook here makes lemon cookies that are delicious but not quite as good as hers.

Your wife,
Emmaline

ADAM READ HIS LETTER AND REREAD IT. HE GRINNED AT THE terrible poetry and rubbed his hand over his mouth, his eyes blinking rapidly. She was fine, and she missed him. He leaned back against the chair and closed his eyes. When had she become his everything? When had he resigned his heart to her keeping? Did he bear the blame for the mess they were in and had she stretched out her displeasure of him with her silence? Yes. Of course. But this was her olive branch.

CHAPTER 14

"I am so excited," Madeline Clair said while seated at the dining room table one evening late November. "I can hardly contain myself!"

"What is it, dear?" her husband asked.

"Yes," Ruth Morton asked from beside Emmaline. "Tell us, Mrs. Clair."

"We have been invited to an evening at the Cassatt home!"

Emmaline looked around the table; many of the other women were wide-eyed and all now talking at once. "Who are the Cassatts?" she asked Violet beside her.

"Oh, this is very exciting! Very exciting! Mr. Cassatt is the president of the Pennsylvania Railroad and very wealthy! One of Philadelphia's first families!" Violet turned her head to Mrs. Clair. "Ma'am? Will his sister be there?"

"I am told the artist, Mary Cassatt, has recently arrived from Paris and will be attending! Oh, ladies! This will be crème de la crème of Philadelphia art society!"

Violet turned to Emmaline. "I must have new evening wear. I simply must. I don't often make such a fuss over my appearance, but I must have a new gown."

"I didn't bring anything quite fancy enough, I don't think, for this party," Emmaline said.

"Then we shall go together to dress shops and have something made. Something lovely and special."

"We shall," Emmaline replied. "We will buy ourselves the fanciest dresses with the most lace, gewgaws, and ribbons there are to be had!"

Dear husband,

I intend to be frivolous this week when I order a costly dress from Shelby's, a very fancy, and expensive, dress shop in Philadelphia. All of us at Clair House have been invited to a party at the home of the owner of the Pennsylvania Railroad, a Mr. Cassatt. His sister, Mary, an artist of some renown, as I am told, will be there and supposedly, all the fanciest folks in the art world. I've spent twenty-two dollars of the five hundred you deposited in my account, but this dress and the shoes and the other accessories will match that amount and more!

I've asked Mr. and Mrs. Clair if you would be able to attend with me and they have assured me that you would be welcome, as Mr. Clair is personal friends with Mr. Cassatt's longtime secretary. I'm hoping you will make the trip. The party is to be held on the second of December at six in the evening and I will attend with Violet if you cannot be convinced to come and will be wearing a lovely silk gown in lavender, the newest style, with bare shoulders and a rather low neckline. I am hoping you will consider visiting.

I miss you.
Your wife,
Emmaline

ADAM CHUCKLED. HE'D RECEIVED FIVE LETTERS FROM Emmaline, and this one sounded like those moments when she'd been at her most natural and confident and funny. Of course, he would go. He had no intentions of allowing a bunch of wealthy Philadelphia men to ogle his wife without being at her side. He went immediately to his desk to reply.

I T W A S A B R I S K , R A T H E R C O L D , S A T U R D A Y A F T E R N O O N , A N D Adam was walking the short distance to Annie and Matt's house, thinking of his trip the following weekend to see Emmaline for the first time in nearly three months. He felt as if he were twelve years old again and waiting impatiently for Christmas morning and all the good food and gifts and visiting that would be done. He could not stop himself from smiling at his response to his wife when he told her he would be very glad to accompany her and just as glad to help her remove that lavender gown when they arrived back at his hotel room after a party where he would most likely have to beat off all of her swains.

Matt and Annie had invited him and Livie and Jim to dinner, as his sister was uncomfortably large in her eighth month. Teddy ran to him when he arrived, and he picked up his nephew and carried him to the dinner table. He could smell roast chicken and was looking forward to having dinner with company rather than alone as he'd been doing. Livie and Jim came in shortly after him, bringing in another gust of chilly air. Matt poured him a glass of wine as Livie helped Ruth into her tall chair and Annie and Sally, their housekeeper, put dinner on the table.

"Who could that be?" Annie said when they heard pounding at the door.

Matt shrugged. "Somebody looking for a good meal, I suppose."

But the door banged open before Sally could touch the knob. Nettie's husband, John, burst into the foyer.

"Adam!" he shouted.

Adam handed Teddy to Annie, and all three men turned to John as he hurried into the dining room.

"Take the children into the kitchen, Sally," Matt said, eyeing John's serious face.

"What is it, John?" Olivia cried. "Has something happened to Nettie? To one of the children?"

He shook his head and looked at Adam. "No. Everyone in Winchester is fine."

"What?" Adam asked. "What has happened?"

"I was in Brunsville a month ago making a delivery. I ran into Carter Nash that day and he asked about our family. I told him that everyone was fine and how excited we were for Nettie's sister to be taken into a fancy school for writers in Philadelphia and about all her successes. I saw him again today when I dropped off something for his order. He told me that coincidentally his cousin Henry headed to Philadelphia yesterday."

"Cousin Henry?" Jim asked.

John let out a held breath. "Nettie believes Henry was the one to get Emmaline in a family way last Christmastime when the three of us attended a party at Carter's."

The blood drained from Adam's face and his heart beat loudly in his chest. "And he's gone to Philadelphia?"

John nodded. "I rode straight away to Paradise to find out you were here at Matt's. I asked Carter if he'd told Henry about Emmaline's success and he said he had when he was with him at a family gathering. I think he's gone there to find her."

"Is it possible it's a coincidence?" Annie asked.

"I don't think so. Carter said that Henry had become agitated when he'd learned Emmaline had married Adam," John said and swallowed. "He also said that Emmaline held a special place in his heart and that he was certain she returned his regard."

"The first train out of Winchester won't be until Monday morning," Matt said.

"There'll be one out of Frederick tomorrow, though," Jim put in.

"That's fifty miles more or less, and twelve hours to do it in," John said, shaking his head.

Adam pulled on his coat. "York will get me there."

"You're not going alone, brother," Matt told him.

"I'm leaving in thirty minutes. Be at Paradise by then if you're coming."

"I'm sorry, Adam. I should have never said anything to Carter," John said. "Do you want me to come?"

"This isn't your fault, and it looks as if you rode hell-bent for leather to get here. You'd best prepare our mother-in-law, and the rest of her family." Adam strode out the door.

"Go, Jim," Olivia said, hurriedly getting his coat. "What are you waiting for?"

"I can't leave you so close to your time."

Olivia began to cry. "You must go! I know you will regret it if you don't. I'll be fine, and John will watch out for me. Go!"

ADAM RAN HOME AND CHANGED INTO THE HEAVY OUTDOOR clothing he wore when working the horses in the winter. He pulled a long canvas coat over top of it all and checked his pistols and knife. He was in the barn talking to George about where he was going and saddling York when Jim and Matt arrived, looking much the same as he did.

"Jim will need a Morgan saddled for this trip, George. Matt has Chester," Adam said calmly. He was forcing himself to think clearly. He couldn't allow himself to become emotional or too excited. There was too much at stake and too many hours until he arrived in Philadelphia.

. . .

"ARE YOU ABLE TO WALK WITH ME THIS AFTERNOON?" Emmaline asked Violet as she leaned against the doorway of her friend's room Monday afternoon. "I definitely need to withdraw money before I pick up my dress at Shelby's tomorrow."

"Certainly. Maybe we can have lunch together first. I did so enjoy that when we went to the Bossler Tea Room. When does the bank close, Emmaline?"

"At three today. We can finish up our classes and be at the tea room by one."

"Perfect!"

Emmaline spent the day thinking about the following weekend and seeing Adam for the first time in months. She couldn't wait. She wanted to permanently remove all the memories of the day of her arrival at Clair House. She wanted new memories with him. She wanted to touch his arm and kiss his mouth. She wanted to spend a lazy Sunday morning with him in bed in his hotel room.

Finally, she and Violet left for the tea room after a particularly arduous morning of classes. She'd have to study late into the evening to make up for her afternoon out. They had just left the bank when a carriage pulled up near them. An older man climbed out.

"Miss Violet," he said.

"Hodges? Whatever are you doing here?"

"Miss Violet. Your father is quite unwell. The doctor is with him now and your mother sent me to Clair House to pick you up."

"Oh! Oh, dear! Father! I must hurry!" Violet's face was pale and worried. She turned to Emmaline. "But we must see my friend back to Clair House."

Emmaline shook her head. "No. That will be in the opposite direction of your home. You must go immediately. I only have a few short blocks to go. Hurry now, Violet."

"I don't know what to do," she said.

"I do. You must go. Hodges? Take Miss Violet to her family right away."

"I think that is the wisest course," he said.

Violet hurried to the carriage and turned back to look at Emmaline. "You will go directly to Clair House?"

"Yes. Now go."

Emmaline watched her friend climb in the carriage and turned into the winter wind for her walk home, glad at that moment to be solitary as she was at a point in her book that she could not decide what the heroine would do. The time it would take to walk the blocks back would be perfect to think it through. Once past the bank and other stores, there were few pedestrians out in the wintry weather and Emmaline pulled her coat tight around her, thankful that Adam had insisted that she buy one.

"Emmaline Somerset! What were the chances that we meet here in Philadelphia?"

Emmaline looked up, startled as she'd been walking into the wind with her chin on her chest. She looked blankly at a young man in front of her until her mind caught up with her eyes.

"Henry?"

"Yes, it's me, Henry!"

He was smiling at her much like she remembered he'd done all that time ago on that fateful night. What a child he was, she thought to herself, compared to her husband.

"What are you doing in Philadelphia?"

"I am going into business. My partner has already established himself in shipping and he has begged me to come aboard with him, as he knows my skills and is paying handsomely for my expertise."

Emmaline quietly harrumphed. "All the best to you then," she said and started to walk past him.

He stepped neatly in front of her. "Oh, wait. Can't we have a bite together, or even just some coffee? It's been almost a year since we've seen each other."

"You knew what town I was from, Henry. You never called, but that was for the best. I wouldn't have received you anyway."

He looked away then out to the street and then back to her. "I heard . . . I heard there were consequences to our kisses that night."

"There were," she said finally, feeling the weight of speaking to the father of that tiny child she'd lost. Would they have been able to form a family together had he known? Would she have been miserable? Most likely.

"Can we at least speak for a few moments in a warmer place? My bag is just here in this doorway. Let me get it and we can find a bakery or restaurant."

She followed behind him a step or two. "No, Henry. There is nothing to say." She turned to walk away.

Henry grabbed her arm. "There is much to say."

"Let me go!"

But before she could say another word, he hustled her through the door of the warehouse. "What are you doing?"

He pulled her along in the near pitch-dark as the door closed behind them. Cobwebs touched her face and hands and she tripped over something. His hand tightened on hers, dragging her forward in the still air, cold and musty.

"You must stop!" she said.

"No, I don't think I will." He pushed her back against the wall and latched his lips on hers.

"Stop!" she cried as she twisted and pulled away from him.

His free hand came up to hold her chin in place, digging into her neck. She tried to bring her knee up against him as Jim had shown her to do, but he had her tightly against the wall. It was at that moment that she gave way a bit to panic, that this man, this horrible boy, might have dangerous ideas about her and there was no one to rescue her. Just as Adam had predicted.

· · ·

"WE MUST LOOK LIKE TEXAS COWPOKES OR RUSTLERS, THE WAY we're dressed, and the way everyone in this station is staring at us," Matt said as he followed Adam down the busy street. "Not too many men carrying guns, either."

"There's a stable," Jim said and pointed. "We're going to have to get a wagon or some horses."

Adam was trying desperately to manage his dread. They'd sat on the train, not moving, somewhere between Frederick and Philadelphia for nearly twelve hours while the tracks were cleared of several fallen trees, and there'd been damage to the engine, too. He'd nearly lost his mind, thinking about Emmaline alone, and had gotten off the train to walk the rest of the distance, until Matt caught him and steered him back on board.

All of his worst fears bubbled to the surface and he couldn't keep himself from envisioning the worst. He thought about his mother facing bandits, frightened and alone. He thought about those few hours holding Josephine's hand while she slipped further and further away from him and how Emmaline might need him right this moment, and he wouldn't be there to hold her hand or save her. He took a deep breath and turned away from his brother and brother-in-law, unwilling to let them see his panic.

They left the stables on three worn-out mounts, Jim's especially struggling under his weight. He wished he had the Morgans with them instead of having to stable them in Frederick and ride these sorry horses, but there was nothing to be done about it. They moved through the busy streets until finally Adam recognized the Bigelow Bank and the hotel he'd stayed at. He spurred his horse faster until they arrived at Clair House. He knocked hard on the door.

Mrs. Mingo answered. "Mr. Gentry?"

"I need to speak to my wife," he said.

"Come in, sir. Let me get Mr. Clair."

Adam stepped into the foyer and waited until Mr. Clair arrived.

"Mr. Gentry? Mrs. Gentry said you wouldn't be coming until later this week."

"Is my wife here?"

"No. She and her friend Violet Dunderson went out to run some errands earlier today. I am surprised they haven't arrived back but sometimes they stop at the bookshop and I believe the time gets away from them when they begin to browse."

"Which way is this bookshop?"

"Near the hotel where you stayed when you first brought Mrs. Gentry to Clair House."

"If she should arrive back, do not let her out of your sight. There is a man who I believe intends to hurt her here in Philadelphia somewhere."

"Oh, my dear," a white-faced Mrs. Clair said from behind her husband. "Someone wants to hurt our Emmaline?"

She slumped against her husband's side as the front door opened behind Adam.

"Miss Violet!" Mr. Clair said. "Where is Miss Emmaline?"

"This is my wife's friend, Miss Dunderson?" Adam asked.

The woman was sniffling into her hanky and swaying on her feet. "I am your wife's friend." She looked up at him, with tears in her eyes.

Adam took her gently by the shoulders, bracing himself for what he knew was a terrible new reality. "What has happened, miss?"

"My father is unwell. I don't believe he will have too many more days on this earth." She turned to Mr. Clair. "I'm going to take some of my clothes home with me today as I'll be staying there indefinitely. I'll make arrangements for the rest of my things to be picked up."

Adam took a deep breath. "I'm terribly sorry to hear about your father, Miss Dunderson, but I believe my wife is in danger. Do you know where she is?"

"Emmaline? In danger? Oh, dear!" she said, wide-eyed and

worried. "My family's retainer found us right after we left the Bigelow Bank. We were on our way home. I wanted to bring her here in our family carriage, but Hodges was most impatient, and she insisted I hurry, in case, in case . . . I didn't want to be too late."

"What time was that, Miss Dunderson?" Adam demanded.

"Hours ago!" she said and began to cry again. "It had to be before three when we arrived at the bank and we were only there a few minutes. Long enough for her to make a withdrawal. It must be five o'clock now, or after. It is nearly dark, and the streetlights are beginning to come on."

"Come on, Adam," Matt said from his side. "We've got to search between here and the bank and see if we can find a clue as to where she's at."

"Mr. Clair?" Adam said. "Please have someone find me if she would turn up here. Leave a message at the Addison if necessary."

"Of course, sir," Clair said, looking only slightly better than his wife, who was crying piteously.

CHAPTER 15

Adam, Matt, and Jim walked down the street toward the bank, three abreast, eyes moving right and left, looking for any clue. Adam was letting himself think the worst and he knew that he shouldn't, that he needed to be clearheaded to search for his wife. But two hours! She'd been gone two hours, and no one knew where she was.

"When should we go to the police department, if Mr. Clair already hasn't?" Jim asked.

"They may be able to help," Matt said. "They may be able to track Nash's movements."

"We don't have time for the police," Adam said.

They walked slowly and in silence then, sharp eyes looking for any trace of Emmaline, the cold wind whipping down the street, blowing leaves and bits of paper in whirlwinds while the gas lamps cast an eerie light.

"Why didn't you tell me about our baby?" Henry asked as she pulled her face from his.

"You never called on me, never came around, and Nettie heard before I even realized I was expecting that you were courting another woman."

"I only saw her twice. She wasn't worth my time."

She very nearly made a remark to him that would certainly anger him, but she sensed that he wasn't completely rational. It was clear to her that she was alone in this and that she would only survive by her wits. If Violet returned to Clair House and realized she'd never come back, they would look for her, but even still, how would they know where to look, and what were the chances that Violet would return, especially if her father was as ill as the retainer had said.

"What was the matter with the woman?" she asked.

"She was a tramp," he whispered close to her ear, making her skin itch and forcing a shiver down her back even as she was tight against a cold brick wall. "She wasn't you. I've heard you've done very well for yourself. You'll make a fine wife for an up-and-coming businessman."

"I'm already married."

"Not for long." He laughed. "Once I get a brat on you again, he'll send you packing. Don't you know the Gentrys are uppity? They don't want a girl who lifts her skirts any old time."

He kissed her then and forced his tongue in her mouth, nearly gagging her. She pushed from the wall with all of her strength and just as she thought she was making progress, he stepped away from her and swung his hand hard in a wide arc. Her head reeled as he smacked her face, bouncing her head off the wall behind her and making her dizzy. Before she could recover her wits, he hit her in the stomach with his fist. She doubled over, gasping for breath. She could taste blood on her tongue and wondered if the crack she'd heard was her rib. He pulled her cloak from her and yanked at her dress. She heard fabric rip and felt cold air on her arm and chest. This man, this horrid little boy, was going to force himself on her. She would fight him to the bitter end.

"Don't do this, Henry. My husband will hunt you down. Don't do this."

He pulled her by the arm across the dim hallway and opened a door she could barely see. He pushed her in ahead of him, releasing her arm, and she heard a lock snick shut. She hurried away from him, barely making out what was ahead of her, and rammed her hip into a table or tall bench. She put her hand down on it to steady herself, heard the chatter of mice, and felt something fur-covered touch her finger. She nearly shouted but swallowed it. When she batted the furry thing away, her fingers brushed something metal, a piece of pipe she realized when she gripped it, like the kind used to move water from a well. A heavy one, maybe three feet long. She picked it up and held it at her side among the folds of her dress.

"There's a pallet over there, Emmaline. Get yourself on it and lift your skirts unless you want me to bust every tooth in your mouth."

If she admitted to herself that she was terrified, she would cry or beg or allow herself to be taken advantage of again, and she just could not do it. She would go with bravado and lure him close enough to swing the pipe and knock him out. "You will have to make me lie down, Henry. I won't do it willingly."

He stalked toward her. She could see the whites of his eyes clearly. He drew back his fist at the same time that she swung the pipe up with all her strength, connecting with his temple with a sickening sound. He reeled in place and she pulled the pipe over her head with both hands prepared to hit him again, but he slumped onto to the floor and wasn't moving. She hurried to the door but couldn't find the knob or the key as she felt around in the dark. She turned her head every few seconds to make sure he was still on the ground. She wondered if she'd killed him. She didn't think she cared.

. . .

ADAM AND MATT WALKED SIDE BY SIDE LOOKING AT THE ground for clues. Jim was across the street asking a man on a bench if he'd seen Emmaline. He looked at them and shook his head. Sweat pooled on Adam's chest and forehead. Cold sweat. The sweat of fear and frustration. He didn't know what else to do and he could sense she needed him.

They were only a block away from the commerce area and Adam believed if this Henry person had a lick of sense, he wouldn't try to steal a woman off the street with merchants and shoppers still around. But he could have dragged her into a carriage easily on this short, deserted stretch. Emmaline wouldn't go down without a fight, though. He closed his eyes, willing himself to stay steady, to find her, to give himself a chance to tell her all things that needed said. He straightened then and shouted at the top of his lungs.

"Emmaline!"

"Adam! Adam! Help me!" he heard faintly.

"Emmaline? Emmaline?" he shouted again.

He and Matt turned to the building behind them where her voice came from, and Jim ran across the street as they went through an open door with a round dirty window. It was dark and dank and cold.

"Emmaline? Where are you?"

Matt shushed him. "Here. I think she's over here."

"Emmaline! We're coming!" Jim shouted.

"I can't find the door lock! Help me before he wakes up!"

"Get away from the door, Emmaline," Adam said and threw himself against the heavy wood, desperate to get to her. He could hear the terror in her voice.

The doorframe began to split and Matt pulled him away. "Let Jim do it. He's got fifty pounds on you."

Adam watched as her brother cracked the thick wood in half the second time he hit it with his body. He went barreling through the opening and fell on the floor. Adam heard moaning but he didn't know who it was, nor did he care, as Emmaline flew through the doorway and into his arms. He held her close, closed his eyes, and sent a prayer aloft.

"I might have killed him," she said then in a breathy, maybe hysterical voice, her eyes wide and wild. "Is he dead?" She lifted up her arm, her hand shaking he could see, with a death grip on a heavy piece of metal.

"Shh," he murmured and moved her toward the door without releasing her. He walked slowly backward, getting her away from whatever had happened. Men in dark uniforms were hurrying down the street with Mr. Clair as the warehouse door closed behind them.

"You've found her!" Mr. Clair shouted.

"Yes," Adam said back and kissed her hair.

She turned out of his embrace, faced the men coming to her in a hurry, one arm clutching her stomach and one arm out at her side still holding the pipe. "I killed him. I think I killed him."

The policemen and Mr. Clair slowed as Adam took his first look at her in the light of the streetlamp. Her dress was filthy and torn, exposing her shoulder and the top of her breast. Her hair was out of its pins and there was blood running down the back of her neck and from the corner of her mouth. He tore off his coat and laid it over her shoulders, bending to pick her up, but she stayed him with her hand and her words.

"There's a man inside on the floor. He fathered a baby on me a year ago. I lost that child before he was born." She pointed to the warehouse door. "He told me . . ."

"Emmaline," her brother said softly. "You don't have to say any of this."

"Yes, I do," she all but shouted.

Adam could hear her shallow breathing and reached for her but dropped his arm to his side. He thought she needed to say whatever it was she was going to say, and she needed to do it on her own, under her own power, just as she'd defeated that bastard Henry. She looked back at the policemen.

"He shoved me against a wall and told me he was going to force himself on me and then he hit me. He dragged me into a room and locked the door. He told me to lie down . . . to lie down and pull up my skirts or he would bust every tooth in my mouth."

Adam's eyes closed, hearing the terror in her voice. "Emmaline, love. We'll sort it out." But she didn't hear him.

"There was a pipe on a bench, this pipe," she said and raised her hand holding it. "When he got close enough to draw back his fist, I hit him with it. I think I killed him and I'm not sorry."

She was shaking and swaying on her feet and Adam couldn't stop himself from pulling her against him. "If you have any more questions for my wife, you may direct them to my attorney or to me. We'll be staying at the Addison Hotel down the street. I'll have a doctor look at her there."

"I just checked on him. He's not dead," Matthew said from behind them. "He's still breathing. I'm hoping he lives so I can kill him."

"Not if I get to him first," Jim said.

She was shaking now in Adam's arms and had closed her eyes. He kissed her forehead. "Our Emmaline has already vanquished the enemy. We have arrived at the end of the story where she is already the heroine."

Her eyelashes flicked, and she looked up at him, seeing him, he thought, perhaps for the first time that evening. "I want a bath and I want to have a long cry, and I don't want to do either in front anyone."

Adam swept her off her feet, turned, and began the walk to the hotel.

* * *

"IF MY MOTHER HAD HUGGED ME ONE MORE TIME," EMMALINE said with a laugh as she leaned against Adam in the gig on their way home to Paradise.

"She's been terribly worried." Adam smiled at her. "She wanted to come to Philadelphia with me several times, and I would have surely brought her, you know. But she didn't right after you were attacked, and then it was only weeks until you were to come home."

She slipped her arm through Adam's. "Mother has never gone far from Winchester. I don't think traveling agrees with her. Your mother came. I think she loves her traveling."

"She does. But what a lovely party your mother had for your homecoming, though," Adam said and smiled.

Snow was coming down and painting the wild landscape white. Emmaline breathed in the cold, crisp forest air. She was longing to see Paradise. Longing to see her home. She'd stayed at Clair House the four weeks following Henry's attack, absorbing every single detail and bit of advice and writing rules she could as she wouldn't be completing the final month there, even knowing there would be nights during those four weeks she would wake alone, in a cold sweat, reliving that terrible evening.

She and Adam had talked about it and decided that she would stay until the Christmas break and he would travel back and forth between Winchester and Philadelphia during that time. She felt better, seeing his face when he came by after classes or in the evening to take her to dinner, just knowing he was close by much of the time, he at his hotel and she at Clair House, although they never did talk about matters as they should have. When he was not in Philadelphia, Mr. Clair was careful to see that she was escorted anywhere she needed to go but she didn't go often. She was happy to heal in the warmth and comfort of Clair House, worrying about her next paragraph rather than an ugly, violent episode that would live somewhere in her head forever.

She and Adam had arrived on the train that morning and went

directly to her mother's and been kissed and hugged and cried over by all, even by Phillip, who had kissed her cheek and told her he was glad she'd conked that bruiser and asked if he could borrow some money now that she was a famous author. Beadle's December addition, which included *Andrew Bartholomew Pans for Gold*, had been released and there were stacks of them on her mother's dining room buffet for her to sign. She'd gotten through the emotional homecoming with no tears but stood very still and quiet when she first saw the book and leafed through it, coming to her story, with her name, Emmaline Gentry, below the title.

Betsy reached for her hands and held them. "I cannot tell you how very proud I am of you. How proud we all are. Daddy would be so pleased."

She hadn't had time to shed any tears with Betsy, though, as John Winders had come up to her and hugged her hard, hard enough that she could barely breathe. He'd sniffed and then whispered in her ear, "I'm so sorry, Emmaline. I'm so sorry I ever said anything."

She'd pulled away from him enough to hold his face in her hands and see that his eyes were suspiciously bright. "It wasn't your fault, John. I was too embarrassed to say it was him and I should have. I should have told you and Nettie right away."

Nettie had leaned in and kissed her cheek and her husband had reached an arm around both of them. "You should have told us but, dear Lord, what if Mother would have made you marry him? You are much better off with Adam, as you well know. Are you teary-eyed, John?"

"No," he'd whispered loudly and run a hand over his eyes. "I've just got something in my eye, is all."

"It's rather charming, you know," Nettie'd said to her husband and raised a brow.

Emmaline had laughed as John shook his head.

"You are ridiculous sometimes, Nettie," he'd said, red-faced, although his eyes never left his wife's.

She'd gotten to hold the newest member of the family when Olivia and Jim had arrived with Emily Somerset, named after Eleanor's sister, who had just woken from her nap. Jim had walked in smiling and carrying the child, holding her as if she were a rare, delicate piece of crystal. He'd reluctantly let Emmaline hold her and Olivia had laughed, looking much like her old self.

"He pays no attention to me any longer since our little Emily arrived," her sister-in-law had said and smiled fondly at him sitting in a chair holding the baby and staring into her wrinkled, scrunched-up face. "Since the moment she was born, it was clear he'd fallen in love with her."

Emmaline sighed happily, thinking of the wonderful welcome she'd had and how satisfying it was to know that they looked upon her as less of an oddity than she'd always feared. The clip-clop of the horses' hooves on the gravel drive alerted her that Paradise was near. She sat up in her seat, feeling a homecoming she couldn't have predicted. This was the place where she would write, where they would raise their children. Where they would comfort each other and rejoice together.

Jenny, Mabel, Beatrice, and George were on the walk waiting for them and she hugged them all and shooed them in the house as the snow was really beginning to come down. There was a decorated pine tree in the main room and she could smell something with cinnamon and sugar baking. Jenny took her new coat, as Adam insisted the one she'd had on that night was beyond repair or cleaning. Adam took her hand and kissed her fingers when the staff had been satisfied that she was home and in one piece.

"Come," he said. "There's something I've been waiting to show you."

"A surprise? I used to like surprises," she said and looked up at him, grinning.

"I think you will like this one." He laced his fingers through hers, pulling her to the staircase, up, and down the long, wide hallway.

They stopped in front of Olivia's bedroom door and he turned to look at her. "I have forever memorized the look on your face when you saw the desk in your room of Clair House that first day. As mad and as upset as we've both been—"

"I was foolish," she interrupted.

He touched his forehead to hers. "No, you weren't, and neither was I. As mad and upset as we'd both been I've spent quite a bit of time thinking of how I could please you as much as that desk did that day. Now cover your eyes."

She chuckled and did as he bid, allowing him to take her elbow and guide her into the room. She dropped her hands, looked around slowly at the fireplace burning brightly, an over-stuffed chair with pillows and a quilt across the back, a full wall of empty bookshelves. But most of all, she stared at a massive, gleaming desk situated between the two windows. She turned to him quickly.

"What? What is this?"

"This is your room. Your office or hideaway. Whatever you want to call it. Where you can come and block out all the comings and goings of Paradise and write to your heart's content." He stepped close to her and cradled her cheek in his hand. "I've been dreaming of this day. Do you like it?"

She nodded. Overcome with all the feelings she'd tamped down, all the desires, all the thoughts that she could just never fit in properly anywhere. She had found her home and found the man that would make it so.

"I love you, Adam. I love you so much I cannot begin to tell you or write it down or even attempt some poetry. I love you. I never thought I would. I never thought we'd be more than companions, but you are my world. I stood there in that cold warehouse with his hand around my neck, and I didn't think of my books or my room or my clothes or anything else other than you. I wanted to live to see you again. I had to because I'd never told you I loved you, and that was a regret I couldn't bear."

He wrapped his arms around her and kissed her deeply. He broke the kiss, staying close enough for her to feel his breath on her face.

"My God, I love you, Emmaline. I was convinced I'd never love anyone again, but I've been granted a reprieve from a life spent in solitude. I love to hear you laugh and watch your eyes light up with wonder. I love that gap between your teeth that makes me want to make love to you at every moment of every day. I've been such a fool thinking I was immune to falling in love with such a talented and courageous woman. I am in awe of you."

ADAM TOOK HER HAND AND LED HER TO THEIR BEDROOM. HE couldn't take his eyes off of her, standing, finally, in the privacy of their room at Paradise. He loved her. He was both joyous and terrified but mostly just wanting his wife. He unbuttoned her blouse, pulling it from her skirt, stopping to kiss her softly. She undid the side buttons of her skirt and then sat down to unhook the buttons on her leather shoes. His back to their bed, he pulled his shirt over his head and yanked off his boots. She stood in front of him in silk drawers and a lace-edged chemise. She looked down at him, below his waist.

"It must know I'm looking at it, even though it is still bundled up in your pants," she said, smiled, and put her hand on his chest, pushing him back until he was stretched out across their bed.

He laughed until she shimmied out of her drawers and pulled the silk underthing over her head, dropping it to the floor. And then his mouth was dry, and his heart was beating loud enough for him to hear it in his ears and he shucked his pants quickly.

"Come here, wife," he said softly.

She lay down on her side, meeting him face-to-face and chest to breast. He ran a hand down her side, down her curves of smooth and silky skin. He leaned forward and kissed her open-mouthed, tangling their tongues and feeling the tips of her breasts dragging against his chest. She looked at him, her eyes drowsy and sensual, drawing her foot up his leg until her knee lay on his hip. His cock brushed against her stomach and the dark hair below it.

"I love you," he whispered and ran a finger down her stomach, and lower, until he found the pulsing warm and wet center of her. She arched her back and moaned.

"Adam," she whispered against his neck. "Oh, Adam."

He reached behind him to his nightstand and the sheath that lay there. She took it from his hand and pitched it over her shoulder.

"Emmaline?"

"Yes, husband," she said and smiled dreamily at him.

"Children will change things for us. For you and your writing."

"I know," she said softly. "I know. I'm going to write all of my life and will have to find a way to have our children and still write my stories or we'll never have any children, and that is the one thing you asked of me when you proposed. I'm ready. Are you?"

Without conscious thought, he rolled her onto her back and pulled her knee around his waist, bringing his cock to the spot it sought. He slid into her then, home, he thought, where all his yesterdays had brought him to and where all his tomorrows would begin. She arched under him and tilted her hips toward him. His wife was sensuous and sexy and fit him perfectly. She smiled then, revealing that gap between her teeth, making him slide in and out of her in a rhythm that they both knew.

He held himself straight on shaking arms looking down at her, at her hair spread across his pillow, at her breasts moving in time with his thrusts, and at her face, at his precious Emmaline.

"I love you," she said. "I love . . . oh, yes, yes, Adam . . ." And they both went away together.

He dropped on to her, their skin sweat-soaked, and rolled onto his back, bringing her with him, her head lying on his chest.

"Do you realize it's the middle of the day?" she asked.

He nodded. "I couldn't wait until nighttime."

"Neither could I." She stretched out like a cat. She giggled, a silly girlish sound that made him look at her. "Do you remember the day you asked me to marry you?"

He nodded. "Of course. Your mother fainted."

"She did, and Phillip asked if she was dead." She looked up at him. "I tried to imagine doing this with you that day. It was silly enough in my head that I nearly laughed at you, but of course I didn't because I was expecting a child and the most handsome, eligible bachelor within a hundred miles was asking me to marry him."

"Laughter would have had a sad effect on my poor self that day." He chuckled.

"This is nothing like I envisioned. There is nothing awkward between us. It is perfect, husband, and I think it will only get better with time."

"And practice," he said and growled, rolling her over and kissing her again and again.

EPILOGUE

1891 Paradise

ELIZABETH GENTRY STOOD IN THE BALLROOM AT PARADISE, watching the dancing, as her family and friends celebrated her grandmother's move back to Winchester, Virginia. Eleanor McManus Gentry had recently married Ian McKellar, both near seventy years old, and moved back to a small house that her father, Adam Gentry, had built for them on Paradise property near the main house. Grandma called it the dower house as if they were in London and her father a duke or an earl. She watched her dearest friend and cousin, Emily Somerset, walk toward her, smiling.

"Have you talked to your father? Uncle Jim can be so old-fashioned," Elizabeth said. "But you look as if you were the cat that stole the cream."

"I have," the eighteen-year-old Emily said. "I am to stay for the whole summer at Aunt Jane's in New York City with her and her husband! I am so excited!"

"I am so glad for you, but I'll miss you so much! What will I do in Winchester for amusement without you?"

"I'm sure you'll find something to amuse yourself with," Emily said and smiled. "Just don't let it be Francis Bridges."

Elizabeth laughed. "Hardly. I have no intentions of tying myself to a Winchester man. Anyway, I want to be through two years of school before the World's Fair in New York."

"What's the matter with Winchester men?" Elizabeth's sixteen-year old brother, Beau, asked. "Anyway, Father is never going to let you go to the World's Fair. Is Uncle Matt wearing a woman's bonnet?"

Emily and Elizabeth turned to look at the other end of the ballroom and watched cousin Ruth walk to them. She was shaking her head and acting as if her father did not exist as he posed in front of the massive marble fireplace.

"Why does he have to embarrass me at every turn?" Ruth said as she joined them. "And your fathers encourage him."

"They do," Emily said. "And so does Uncle John. I can imagine the four of them getting into trouble when they were young boys, and I'll bet my allowance that Uncle Matt was the ringleader."

"Stop leering at Mrs. McDonagle, Beau," Elizabeth said to her brother when she noticed him staring intently over his shoulder.

He shrugged. "Her gown is very nice. That's what I was looking at."

Emily and Ruth laughed.

"Her gown is nice?" Elizabeth said. "You mean her gown is cut low in the bosom!"

Beau turned back to his cousins, his face flushed. "Stop talking about it, sis. Or I'll tell Father about your wild plans to go to the World's Fair."

"Don't you dare, you sneak. I'll get Mother on my side first and then she'll manage Father when the time comes. Perhaps I'll tell them about your plans."

"Shush!" Beau said. "It will crush father when I eventually tell him, and I really don't like the idea of disappointing him."

"About this degree in medicine?" Edward strolled up and asked.

"Quiet! You're worse than my sister, Edward," Beau said to his cousin and closest friend.

"Well, someone is going to have to manage the Paradise Stables. If Elizabeth is going on a whim to a World's Fair and you're going to medical school, perhaps it will be Eleanor." Edward nodded across the room. They turned in unison to Elizabeth's eleven-year-old sister, in a chair in a corner, with her shoes off and her feet under her, reading a book and completely ignoring the party going on all around her.

"Maybe Edwina?" Emily asked.

Elizabeth laughed. "It will have to one of them and Edwina is the more likely choice."

"Just like Teddy will be taking over our lumber mill and Edward is destined to sell pneumatic tires for horseless carriages since Uncle Jim and Aunt Olivia invested in that company," Ruth said.

"There is Grandma and Mr. McKellar," Edward said. "Come along, Beau. I want to talk to talk to him about Washington."

Emily and Elizabeth watched their brothers and cousin Ruth drift to the crowd now gathered where the Gentry matriarch, Eleanor Gentry, arrived looking every bit as dignified, beautiful, and gracious as she always had.

"What will you do at the World's Fair?" Emily asked. "You know your parents will protest and insist that you not go or that you must be chaperoned. You will not even be twenty years old when it occurs. I mean, what do you want to see or do or learn that will be important enough to argue with them, or even defy them?"

Elizabeth turned to her cousin and smiled. "I want to see and do everything possible. And I intend to do just that. I am a Gentry after all."

THE NEXT GENERATION OF GENTRYS AND SOMERSETS:
Annie and Matthew Gentry
Teddy (1870), Ruth (1872), and Mary (1885)

JIM AND OLIVIA SOMERSET
Emily (1873), Edward (1875), twins Vincent and Benjamin (1879)

ADAM AND EMMALINE GENTRY
Elizabeth (1874), Beauregard (1875), Eleanor (1880), and Edwina (1881)

NETTIE AND JOHN WINDERS
Rachel (1869), Albert (1871), and John (1874)

FROM THE AUTHOR

Thank you for purchasing *For Her Honor*, the fourth and final installment in the **Gentrys of Paradise** series. I hope you enjoyed it. The novella, *Into the Evermore,* is the first book of the series and tells the story of Eleanor and Beauregard Gentry's meeting and marriage. The next book, *For the Brave*, is Matt Gentry's story and how Annie Campbell saved him from a spring flooded river and his own demons. *For This Moment* is the third book and chronicles Olivia Gentry's coming of age as she must choose between a marriage with a man she'll never love or pining for a family friend she's loved since she was a young girl.

The Browns of Butcher's Hill is my newest series of historical mysteries set in Baltimore and begins with *Kidnapped*, followed by *Blackmailed*, and *Murdered*. Follow working man, Phillip Brown as he untangles mysteries in the lowest to the highest with the help of Virginia Wiest, daughter of the owner of the Wiest Cannery, where Phillip is employed.

My series, **The Thompsons of Locust Street**, begins with *The Bachelor's Bride* and are the stories of an unconventional family taking Philadelphia high society by storm. The second book in the series is *The Bareknuckle Groom* followed by *The Professor's Lady*, *The Captain's Woman* and recently released *The Earl's Match*. An excerpt of the *The Bachelor's Bride* follows!

The Crawford Family series remains popular and includes, *Train Station Bride, Contract to Wed, The Maid's Quarters*, and *Her Safe Harbor*. This series details the lives of three wealthy Boston-born sisters. Standalone, historical romance, *Romancing Olive,* chronicles the life of a sheltered Philadelphia spinster as she heads west to save a niece and nephew. *Reconstructing Jackson* is the story of Reed Jackson, crippled confederate officer, who moves west to begin again, post-Civil War. *Cross the Ocean* is a British Victorian-era romance and my general fiction titles, *Politics & Bedfellows* and *All the News* are also available at all of your favorite stores under the name Hollis Bush.

If you enjoyed *For Her Honor*, please post a review or share your thoughts with friends and family. News about my books is available at my website, hollybushbooks.com and ebooks can be purchased directly from that site. I post regularly on my Face-Book page with excerpts from all my books and I welcome you to follow me on Threads at @hollybushbooks. Thank you again for your purchase!

THE BACHELOR'S BRIDE
EXCERPT

Meet the Thompsons of Locust Street, an unconventional family taking Philadelphia high society by storm...

Philadelphia 1868

Chapter One

"No! No, you will not, James."

"I will do as I wish," he thundered, slamming his hand on the thick wooden table, making the crockery dance.

"I am the head of this family, and I say you will not breathe a word of this to our brother or sisters," Muireall Thompson said through gritted teeth.

"Head of the family, are you, lass?"

"I am the oldest."

"And a *real* sibling to boot," James said and marched out of the kitchen.

Elspeth hunched under the stairwell outside the kitchens and watched her brother hurry past, his leather boots slapping against the stone floors, nearly masking his whispered curse words. He slammed the door at the top of the steps. She jumped when Aunt Murdoch spoke to her, just inches from her ear.

"What are you doing, child?" she asked.

"I was eavesdropping on an argument between Muireall and James."

"Does anything good ever come from eavesdropping?"

"Nay. Never," Elspeth said. "But that won't stop me from doing it."

One side of Aunt's mouth turned up. "There's no denying you're a MacTavish, with that sassy tongue of yours."

"MacTavish, Aunt? I've heard you call one of us that on occasion, but I never understood why. Are they our ancestors? A clan we'd best forget?"

"Shush," Aunt Murdoch hissed. "Have you finished the mending? Or are you just lazing about, listening to others' private talks?"

Elspeth looked into Aunt Murdoch's filmy blue eyes. There were some mysteries surrounding her family, the Thompsons. Some secrets. She'd overheard snippets over the years as some had not realized she was in the same room with them, but lips immediately clenched when they did realize, or when her younger sister, Kirsty, or her younger brother, Payden, were nearby. Aunt knew all the secrets, she was certain, but she was just as certain that she would never reveal any of them.

"I need more blue thread to fix one of Kirsty's church dresses. I'll be going to Mrs. Fendale's for more."

"Then get there and get back," Aunt said and went through the door to the kitchens, no doubt to harass Muireall.

Elspeth found James in the parlor, repairing the floor where a nail had come up through one of the varnished boards.

"If you pound that any harder, you're going to fall through," she said, wondering what he could have possibly meant by *real sibling* when he was arguing with Muireall.

"Better than fighting with our sister," he said, each word punctuated by a pound of the hammer. He sat back on his heels and looked up at her as she pulled on her short linen jacket. "Where are you off to?"

"Mrs. Fendale's for thread."

"You shouldn't be going to that part of town alone," James said as he stood. "I have to see about this beet delivery today, but I'll take you tomorrow."

"I'll be fine, James," she said to his sputtering. She stopped at the front door and pulled on her bonnet, examining herself in the mirror above the marble table. James was still telling her she wasn't allowed to leave without him, as she was a stubborn and foolish girl, when she pulled the door closed behind her.

She set out north toward the edge of Society Hill where they lived, crossing Chestnut Street, enjoying the spring air. Streets were crowded with carriages and wagons and horses, and all types of people too. Elspeth's family knew their neighbors, and she waved at old Mrs. Cartwright sweeping her steps and watched Mr. Abrams shaking his finger at his children as their heads nodded in agreement. The sun was shining, one of the first March days to be warm, and it seemed as though everyone was out of their homes and enjoying the weather after a particularly long and cold winter.

Three blocks more and she was less likely to wave or shout a hallo. She stared straight ahead, glimpsing the swinging sign over the door of her destination, and did not listen to the ridiculous and inappropriate comments some young men were directing at her. In just their shirtsleeves, no jacket or four-in-hand tie, and even some without a vest, they were hanging about a stairwell to a basement or coal chute or leaning against the gas streetlight posts, hooting and hollering at each other and at others on the street. Once she crossed Arch Street into Southwark, the houses were a little shabby, the streets had a little more garbage strewn about, and the residents looked a little more downtrodden, but she could see Mrs. Fendale's Millinery shop, not half a block away.

Unfortunately, she'd have to pass the bawdy house—not that she was supposed to know it was a bawdy house or even know what a bawdy house was, but she did have ears and a brain between them and would have been hard-pressed not to understand the conversation she'd overheard between James and his friend MacAvoy. But as it was just ten in the morning, hopefully those ladies would still be abed. It was quiet as she passed by, with one lone woman hanging out a second-floor window in a sheer chemise, one shoulder strap hanging down her arm, with a shiny corset over top of it, which was scandalous enough, but it was red —bright, blood red! All satin and lace and nothing like her own white cotton undergarments. She wondered why a woman would want to wear such a thing, but then, with a second glance at the woman, now smiling at her and tapping a thin cigar against the brick sill, she knew. It would entice a man, but what kind? Surely not a good one! Elspeth shivered and hurried her steps.

A bell rang over her head as she entered the seamstress's shop. "Hello, Mrs. Fendale! How are you this beautiful spring day?"

"Miss Thompson! How good to see you after this long winter! What may I help you with? A new hat, perhaps?"

Elspeth shook her head. "Oh no. I'm just doing some mending and have run out of blue thread." She ran her fingertips over lace lying out on the glass-top counter. "How beautiful! Maybe I will take a yard or two of this to add to Kirsty's best dress."

"It's a very lovely lace, made right here in our neighborhood," Mrs. Fendale said with a smile. "How much shall I cut for you?"

"I think two yards. It will be perfect to liven up one of last year's dresses."

While Mrs. Fendale tied the cut ends of the lace and wrapped the purchases, her son Ezra came out from between the dark hanging curtains that led to the back of the shop where the seamstresses and hatmakers worked. His head dipped into a nod as he smiled shyly, and a blush crept up his face.

"Good morning, Ezra." Elspeth smiled at the younger man.

"G-G-Good morning, Miss Thompson," he said and swallowed.

"Here, Ezra." Mrs. Fendale handed her packages to him. "Carry Miss Thompson's things for her until she crosses the street."

"I'll be fine, Mrs. Fendale. No need to take Ezra away from whatever work he's doing for you."

"His work will still be here when he returns, and I'll feel better knowing he's with you until you've passed this block," she said and shook her head. "To think that those hussies ply . . ." Mrs. Fenway glanced at her wide-eyed son and then at Elspeth and closed her mouth.

"Good day to you, Mrs. Fenway, and thank you," Elspeth said with a smile.

"Good day, Miss Thompson."

Ezra followed her out of his mother's shop, holding the wrapped lace under his arm. "You needn't walk behind me, Ezra." She took the lace from his hands and put it in her bag along with the thread.

The young man hurried to walk beside her, keeping pace with her swift stride. Elspeth tilted her face to the sun, feeling its warmth, letting it seep into her muscles and make her feel as if all things she'd dreamed of were possible. That pleasurable feeling did not last long.

"Get your hands off me, you filthy copper," a woman shouted.

Elspeth looked up at the doorway of the bawdy house she was nearing. There was an older man, with mutton chops and a nearly bald head, being dragged out the door by a younger man in a dark suit. The woman who had shouted, the one in the chemise and red corset Elspeth had seen earlier, was hanging on to the bald man's sleeve, trying to drag him back inside the brick row house. There were no policemen in sight, but a crowd had gathered, mostly consisting of the young men who'd taunted Elspeth on her walk to Mrs. Fenway's.

"'E ain't going nowheres until 'e 'ands over me fee," she screamed and yanked on the bald man's jacket. Elspeth heard a ripping sound. The woman reached around the bald man and kicked at the younger man with a pointy-toed shoe.

"Ouch," he said and rubbed his thigh with his loose. "Let go of him, and I'll pay you."

The woman spit at the younger man, and the bald one found his footing and cuffed the woman hard across the face. She crumbled to the stoop with a cry, holding her face in her hands.

"Fucking whore telling me what to pay," the red-faced bald man shouted to cheers from the crowd of popinjays.

The woman looked up from where she cowered, and Elspeth could see blood running from her nose and lip. She'd seen enough.

"Stop!" she shouted as she picked up her skirts and hurried up the steps. "Stop this instant!"

Elspeth crouched down and pulled a handkerchief from her drawstring bag. She handed it to the woman, who looked up at her guardedly. Elspeth leaned forward and dabbed the blood from the woman's chin and mouth while the young men on the street in front of the house continued their taunts. She stood quickly and turned to the bald man.

"Pay her! Pay her this minute," she said.

The young man stepped between them. "There's no reason for you to get involved, miss. Please be on your way."

She batted his hand away when he reached for her. "Don't you dare touch me! You and your . . . your father are here together? How disgusting you are!"

The crowd roared their approval, and she could see Mrs. Fenway and Ezra at the edge of the crowd. The shop owner said something to her son, and he raced down the street, away from his mother's shop.

"This is not my . . ." the young man said, clearly affronted.

"Then why are you here with him? What need do you have to frequent this house?"

The young man's mouth twitched, and that was when she noticed he was startlingly handsome. Strikingly so. The crowd on the street was taunting him, asking him to tell her about his need. She felt her face go red and wished she could have taken back her words, but it was too late. She would have to brazen it out and was about to repeat her question when the bald man leaned close to her.

"What do you know of this house, girl? Are you looking to audition? I'll be happy to recommend you if you meet my expectations." He let his eyes drift down to her bosom and farther still.